Alone
In The
Darkness

By

MATTHEW BUZA

Copyright © 2016 by Matthew Buza.

For information contact: www.matthewbuza.com

Book and Cover design by Matthew Buza
Book edited by Arial Buza and Emer Gary
Additional thanks to B. Allen Thobois

ISBN-10: 0692693254
ISBN-13: 978-0692693254

First Edition: April 2016
Second Edition: July 2016
Third Edition: April 2018

10 9 8 7 6 5 4 3

Thank you for taking the time to read my book. I hope you enjoy the journey. When you are finished please take a moment and head back to Amazon and give me a review. It really helps me to establish myself and for others to find the book. Please head over to my website to sign up for my mailing list and check out what other books I have available. I wish you the best.

www.matthewbuza.com
www.amazon.com

For my wife and daughter.

Through the river
Draped in water
Hands slide on pebbles
My eyes are dark
I pray for home

CHAPTER ONE

The red evening sky peeked through the clouds and flowed through the city of Everett out along Ebey Island. The river split cupping the island dotted with homes and wire fenced pastures. The island levy was barely visible from the hill above where the man stood next to his car thumbing a cigarette nervously in the light drizzle. Behind the man came the night pouring through the Cascades.

He pulled out his phone swiped quickly with his thumb. The message still said *delivered*.

The man paced around his car, thumbing through his contacts selecting a number and brought the phone to his ear.

"Hello," the phone answered.

"George, it's Steven."

"What's up, man? You want to come over tonight?"

"No, I can't. Actually, I'm in a tough spot. I owe some money and I need a little help."

"How much do you owe?"

"A couple thousand. "

George's voice couldn't hide his surprise, "Who do you owe it to?"

"Hector and his crew." There was silence on the line.

"Shit." George's voice sounded like the air had been taken out.

"I know man, it's bad." Steven's head dropped to the ground and then back up as traffic passed by. Vehicle headlights illuminated his car. His shadow stretched along the brambles and out over the cliff.

"Steven, I…" He paused for a moment, "I don't know if I can help right now. I'm out of cash and the stamp money won't kick in for a few days. How soon do you need it?"

"I need to make a delivery tonight."

"Is there anything you can pawn? Can you talk to your mom?" Steven winced.

"I turned in what I could and scraped together a little money, but I still need more. I've moved some of the product, but I've got more."

"Damn, why did you get in with that guy? You have a good thing going on right now."

"I know, I was dumb. I was speaking with one of his street guys one day and it sounded like a sure thing. I thought I could move some on the side and no one would know. "

"How much do you have left?"

"About 10 bags of Meth."

"That's not much. How much did you pull down?

"Shared some with some people and moved a little."

Steven could feel George's disappointment on the other side of the line. He had known George since high school and it burned to think of involving him. George questioned Steven, "How soon do you need it?"

Steven paused, "I'm not sure. I sent a message to Juan asking for more time."

"Man, I will see what I can do but I don't think I will be able to help. I'll check to see if anyone might want your excess. I'll let you know if I hear anything. I'm sorry." Another pause, "Be safe, these are not good guys."

Steven let his breath out as he spoke, "I know, thanks for the help."

He brought the phone to his side and stared back towards town. A light mist fell around him. He walked around and got into the car and reached down under the dash pulling on a hidden compartment. He removed the bags and rolled them in his hands. The green light of the dash illuminated his face in the failing evening light. He had been in tight situations before, but this was the first time he felt this type of pressure.

The door closed and he slumped into his seat. He mouthed to himself, *Think, think, think.* He pulled out his phone and began to type the same message to a wave of contacts, *I have some ice I need to move. Any takers?*

He sat back and rubbed his hand repeatedly on his pants as if trying to remove something unseen. His fingers crooked like claws. He needed help focusing so he reached into his jacket and pulled out a small glass pipe and laid it on his lap. He reached for a small metal plate near the dash and removed the knife from his jacket, opening the blade. He pulled out a small bag and placed the translucent rock onto the plate. With the butt end of the knife, he ground the rock into a fine powder. He pulled a small straw out from the dash, filled the bottom end and placed it into the glass bulb. He raised the bulb to his mouth with the lighter underneath.

His phone lit up and buzzed, *I'll take some.*

Steven's eyes closed. He opened the flame and rocked back and forth under the bulb. His mind shrank to the green swirl of the flue. He rocked the lighter over the bulb ensuring even heating. The powder slowly began to melt into a clear liquid. A light smoke began to lift from the bulb and Steven began to pull. His lungs filled. He could feel the burn and held it in. 1 second, 2 seconds, 3 seconds. Out. He placed his lips on the glass piece and pulled again. The smoke pulled into his lungs, entering his body, racing to his heart and mind. He lowered the bulb to his lap. His eyes opened to the world clear and smooth.

Another buzz and the light from his cell phone, *If you have something I'm interested.*

Steven leaned back. He could feel the rush and he began to focus. The minutes rolled off as he sat in the car. He checked his phone messages and scrolled past the junkies and meth heads; there was one message that mattered, and that was from Juan. The message was clear and it was marked *Read*. His eyes drifted from the screen empty and wishful. He could only imagine the discussion occurring on the other side of that text, *Read*. That tenuous link over the digital distance. Meaning and mystery. What could they be thinking and would he get the time to make things right?

The screen turned black and then began to buzz. the name *Juan* appeared on the front. Steve let out his breath as he pulled back into reality. His thumb hovered over the red button on the screen. At this moment he was overwhelmed with hope and fear. The phone buzzed again. He pressed and pulled the phone to his ear.

"Hello."

"It's Juan." As if Steven hadn't seen that on his phone.

"Hey man, did you get a...did you get my text?"

"I'm sitting here thinking. I've got a lot to do today. One of those things is you walking up to me and placing an envelope of cash into my hand. I would then count that cash. Look up at you and then smile saying 'Thank you for your business, Amigo' and then watch you leave."

"Yea..."

"And then you would walk back to your car, get in, and drive off."

"Yea..."

"And I would then go back to Hector and say, 'That Steven guy paid up' and we could all have a beer. But in reality, I'm sitting here, with lots on my mind, and my phone tells me that you're off probably smoking up the stash, shitting your pants, hovering over a keyboard asking for more time. This makes me upset."

"I just wanted to know if I could hold off until tomorrow."

"Steven...you're free to hold off until tomorrow. That is fine. Your choice, my friend."

Steven leaned back with a small smile and let out a breath, "Thank you." He could feel the pressure lifting. Another day might be all he needed.

"You're free to do that. And when you're sleeping tonight it will be my choice on how I am going to scatter you across this county." There was a pause as the word *scatter* hung in the air. "Tonight at 11 pm you will be here in front of my house handing me cash. By the look of it you have just over three hours."

Steven's chin hit his chest.

"Steven?" There was a pause. "Steven?"

Steven could barely open his lips. It was dry and his tongue was sticking to the roof. "Steee...ven?"

Steven licked his lips. "Yeah."

"Steven. I need you to acknowledge what I just said."

"I hear you."

"11, Steven." The call ended. There was a silence in the air and he couldn't breathe. His body was frozen in fear. The car sat motionless in the light rain. From the road, the lights showed on the brambles as cars and trucks drove by. Steven began to punch the steering wheel and scream into nothingness. The sound of his screams and the screech of the horn were drowned out by people rushing by, trying to get home for the evening. Ahead of the car, a valley opened up to an island wrapped by a river and in the distance, a city on the sound. A city that offered Steven no peace.

CHAPTER TWO

Steven calmed himself, wiping the spit from his steering wheel and running his face along his jacket. He plugged his phone in and placed the keys in the ignition and turned. The car roared to life and music began to stream from the speakers. He flipped up a cigarette and lit it while the driver side window rolled down. It was nearly dark and his evening was just beginning. He knew there might be a chance he could pull this off but his time was melting away. The evening light was quickly fading as he pulled onto the highway junction and merged onto Highway 2 heading west to Everett. His eyes narrowed as the steady stream of lights headed east in the opposite direction. The song changed and the rain increased streaking across the window with the windshield wipers floating hypnotically.

The city lights built as he merged onto Hewitt Avenue stopping at a light and then turned right onto Broadway. It was a Friday night and the street was lined with shuffling faces moving amongst the pawn shops and tobacco stores. The city is located north of Seattle on a narrow strip of hill boarded by the river and the sound, filled with old homes and even older streets.

Steven turned off Broadway onto quiet neighborhood streets with cars guarding the borders. Rows of identical houses flowed by as Steven glanced out the open window to the backlit clouds. A reflection of the city life lay behind. Steven flicked the remainder of his cigarette and the sparks exploded on the pavement below. He turned left and then pulled into an open parking space.

Steven quickly grabbed his things and exited the car. He walked up to the sidewalk and made his way down to a faded red home with a broken porch railing.

From Steven's left, he heard a cry, "Hey, Steven my man!"

Steven nodded with a short wave as he entered the house. The floors creaked under his hollow steps. Steven crossed the entry and onto the well-worn carpet that contained years' worth of dirt and dust.

"Welcome home," said a cold voice.

Steven ignored the voice and kept his head down passing by the living room.

"Arentcha gonna to say hello to your motha." The words slurred from her chapped lips as Steven continued around the corner and entered the stairs taking steps two at a time pulling with his arms in an effort to leave the voice in the distance.

"You going to say something to your mom?" Her boyfriend's voice chased Steven up the stairs. His hands thumbing a rubber elastic band. He lovingly moved his hand across the sores on the woman's face brushing her hair over her ear.

"You see, I tell you, no respect." She glanced back at the man and then down to the band. "No respect." A smile came to her mouth.

Steven reached the landing and turned to the lit room. He burst in to see a young man on the floor with headphones on and fingers smashing the game controller, eyes glued to the screen where a rifle was zoomed to a face. The button was smashed and a light red mist released on screen, a smile moved across the boy's face. Steven shut the door alerting his brother to his presence. The game was paused and the headphones lowered, "What are you doing here?"

"Ryan, I don't have any time right now. Do you have any money I could borrow for a day?"

"What are you talking about?"

"Money, I need money right now. Do you have anything?"

"Goddammit Steven. What's the rush, man?"

"Ryan, I'm good for the money. I just need a little help. I promise I'll get you paid back as soon as possible. I wouldn't ask this if I didn't need it"

Ryan took a deep breath, he knew there was no fighting his brother. It would either end in him handing over cash or it would be beaten out of him. Tonight he decided the look in his brother's eyes was desperate enough to take the easier road. He resigned himself and slowly rose from the carpet and walked over to the headboard of the bed. He grabbed the golf club from the corner and pulled back on the wooden frame. He reached down hooking a plastic bag and lifting. Ryan lowered the bag onto the bed. He pulled out the small tin and opened it. Inside was a deck of cards and some cigarettes. Ryan dumped out the cigarettes and reached into the pack pulling out a wad of green bills.

"Thank you."

"How much do you need?"

"How much do you have?"

"About 500."

"I need it all."

"Are you kidding me? What do I use for change tomorrow? Am I telling people, 'Sorry sir, only exact change today?'"

"I need it all." Steven took a step forward and Ryan pulled back slightly. There was a tense pause as options ran through Steven's mind. His eyes widened, "Ryan, I'm asking you for a favor. I am in deep shit and I need that cash."

Ryan's eyes lowered to the cash and he extended his arm. Steven grabbed the money and thumbed it quickly. Just over 500. He placed the cash into his pocket.

"Thanks." Steven slumped to the bed and sat down. "Do you have a joint in here? I've got to come down, I'm riding too high."

"Yea, I can see that. You look like you're panicking."

Ryan walked over to his dresser and pulled out a small tin and opened it. He pulled out the small white stick and passed it to his brother. Steven quickly put it into his mouth and opened his lighter. He took a long drag and passed it to his brother. They shared the joint and Steven closed his eyes off to the world. They shared no sound.

Steven rose from the bed and pointed to his brother's pinched fingers, "Add that to my tab."

He exited the room and walked down the hall and through the door at the end. His room was stale and musty. He spent little time here preferring to crash on various couches or pull into a rest stop and lean back in the car. He had spent his entire life moving in and out of this doorway down the same hall avoiding the first floor of his house. Crossing the barrier of the room imparted some peace into his mind. For the longest time when he was young, it was a refuge, a place he could escape the sounds and sights.

He moved to a sagging shelf and pulled out three books and tossed them onto the bed behind him. He stepped over a pile of clothes and pulled out the top drawer emptying the socks and boxers onto the floor below. He pulled the taped wad of money from the bottom of the drawer and slid it back into the dresser. He then crossed the room and pushed the door and hopped up onto a small chair. He carefully detached the air vent frame from the wall and reached deep into the duct. He pulled out a small container. He returned to the bed and began to count the cash. He pulled the money from his jacket pocket and assembled his complete stash. "2500."

His phone buzzed on the bed, *up if u got some.*

Steven grabbed the phone and furiously began responding to the messages. *Leaving now will be there soon. Quarter Gs at 150. Cash only.*

Over Steven's shoulder, two peering eyes showed through the door opening, eyeing the money on the bed and his brother furiously typing away on his phone. Steven stood up and pulled back the covers on the bed and reached shoulder deep. He emerged with a black pistol, his beloved HK. A quick twist of his hand and he pulled the clip out, set it on the bed and checked the chamber. He inserted the clip back in, clicked the safety and slid the gun into his pant pocket. His brother entered the room.

"Where are you going with that?" There was a fear in his voice.

Steven's head did not leave the bed as he collected the money and the metal tin.

"I've got some business to attend to and a debt to pay off. I need you to pretend you didn't see this." His head turned and his eyes met his brothers in an effort to communicate the gravity of the situation. There was a darkness in the eyes as his brother slowly shook his head. "Please head back to your room and play your games. Make sure you get out of here tonight. Go somewhere, anywhere, I don't care. You promise?"

"Yes."

Steven's phone buzzed again. His eyes glanced at it and the name sucked him in, *Juan.*

Hey amigo, working hard to get the money? 11 Steven. There was an image attached. He swiped to open, it was of his house with the lights on in the upstairs rooms. Steven shot to the window and opened the curtains. Ryan stepped back against the wall.

Steven looked out the window and saw a black Mustang with blue stripes under lighting driving down the street. It hit the corner and the back end swung around. The neighborhood was shaken as the car accelerated down the street.

"Was that them?"

"Just make sure you're out of here tonight. Go to a friend's house or something."

Ryan stood there staring at his brother whose head fell down. He could see the weight of the moment on his shoulders. "Alright."

"Make sure you wear a hood and leave by the back. Don't take the streets, slide out via the alleys and keep your head down."

Steven turned and dug through the small tin. He pulled out a small bag of old weed and tossed it to his brother, "Payback for the blunt."

He pulled out two bags of Coke and put them into his jacket.

"I'll text you tonight around 11 if things are good." Steven pulled up the money, rolled it with a rubber band, lifted his foot on the bed and tucked the cash into his sock. He walked past his brother and down the hall. Ryan stood in the room looking out the window.

Steven slid down the stairs and hit the floor below. To his right he saw his mother and her boyfriend swaying in the center of the room, their arms draped over each other's shoulders and their eyes rolled back as exotic music played on the stereo. They were both miles away and never saw him leave the house.

He left the front porch and crossed the yard. He walked up to the neighbor, "Do you need some ice tonight. I've got quarters. 200?"

The man on the porch reached into his pocket and pulled out cash, "I've got only 150."

"Deal."

"Text me if you know of anyone who needs a hit tonight. I'll be free until 10:30." Steven took the cash and slipped the man a small clear bag. He walked down the sidewalk and got into his car. He pulled away towards the hospital. There are always customers near the hospital.

CHAPTER THREE

Steven spoke into the phone, "Hello."

"Hey," a muffled voice spoke. "I got, I got your text message. Do you still have some left?"

"Yes. Are you still located at the same place?"

"Yes, we're in that same house, but we've moved to the unit on the right. Number 334. Just come in when you get here."

Steven glided down the grass. He knew the man on the phone had been a good buyer in the past. But he was an odd buyer, someone who was on the tail end of the meth curve, someone who used more than they should and looked it. He could remember scabs, lots of scabs, and a twitch in the eye, always moving never sitting still. It was a side effect of too much high-quality product or something homemade.

"Alright man, I'll be there in a few minutes. I'm only taking cash tonight. No swaps like last time." Steven jingled the gold swap on his left wrist. He still had time.

"Cash. No problem. I've got that. We'll be here, number 334. Just come in. We will be here."

Steven could hear another voice on the phone, distant, but definitely a female voice. She seemed to be talking to the man but he couldn't make it out over the street noise as he walked down from the apartment complex.

"See you then."

He brought the phone down from his ear. It was dark now, only the city provided guidance. Lights bounced off the low clouds, streetlights flickered, and traffic ebbed and flowed. He was getting to his goal, just over a grand away. A few more stops in the city and he would be free.

Steven fell into the car. He fumbled in his pocket and pulled out the fresh cash. He reached under the seat and pulled a small lever. A money roll fell out into his hand. He pulled the rubber band off and wound in the new hundreds. He lifted it to his nose and took a long drag, a slight smile came across his mouth. He tapped the wad twice on the steering wheel, wrapped the band, and placed the roll back into the compartment.

Steven paused a minute, checking his mirrors. The road noise rang and an old homeless man pushed a cart along the sidewalk, bags hanging from the side and talking at the brick wall passionately conversing with the graffiti. He seemed upset and Steven could hear him talking about something that was his and not to take it from him. Steven smiled, "I got you, old man." He pulled away down the street.

His phone rang. He could hear it buzz to his right and his right eye could see the light coming from the bucket seat. Steven waited and thought twice about looking down at the phone. He was fresh with cash, a couple thousand dollars. He could head down the street, merge onto the freeway and drift off to a new place. He could set up east of the mountains or maybe head into Idaho. Thoughts of running away always filled his mind. From an ocean front condo in San Diego to an isolated cabin in the Bitterroot mountains. He craved the feeling of a fresh start, leaving open wounds behind. Life had become stale and one of these days he thought he would do it. He blinked and looked down, *Mark*. It was better than he thought.

He pressed the accept button on the steering wheel and he spoke to the road ahead of him, "Mark, what's up?"

"You're on tonight."

"On for what?"

"You're cooking with Tyler and the crew tonight."

"No, no, I'm not scheduled for this week, I have it off."

"We've had a dropout tonight and we need you to swap in." Steven shook his head.

"Don't shake your head."

"I'm not."

"I know you're shaking your head. "

Steven slowed to the red light. "When am I needed?"

"At 11. You've got some time to get your shit together and head out."

Steven bit his lower lip and gave the steering wheel a palm smash. He pulled away from the light.

"I've got some errands I'm trying to finish up and I won't be done until after 11."

"Fine. I'll tell Tyler you will be a little late. We've got a large processing run to complete tonight. The Boss has requested we refill inventory for the North end and Eastside. You'll be at the valley house east of Arlington. One of the regular homes."

"That house is garbage. I hate working out there."

"I've taken that note. We'll see you after 11. Later."

The phone clicked as he pulled up to the red light. A woman in a black Ford Explorer rolled up next to Steven and looked across her shoulder. The rapid movement and the screaming drew her attention as Steven pounded his fists on the wheel. Her eyes opened wide and she couldn't help but smile. Her face turned a green hue and she left the man in his misery.

CHAPTER FOUR

Steven stood in the living room carefully avoiding the filth around him. The walls were a dirty yellow color from years of captured smoking. The corners of the room contained pockets of mold peeking in from the long Pacific Northwest winters. The room contained a couch with torn cushions and stained pillows. The sole light source was a shade-less lamp in the corner pumping out a dull orange light that extended gangly shadows onto the walls. The dark corners and lines provided ideal hiding locations for nightmares to fester. He fought the musty smell that permeated the air, but there was no giving in. His lungs burned as he inhaled. He knew this smell, the last few years of dealing baptized him to this. It was the merging of neglect and lack of human hygiene. More than anything else, Steven hated meth dens. These were the worst places to go, filled with the lowest of the low. The poor souls resting inches from the edge, peering over a needle or pipe into the abyss below. Steven needed the money and he needed it now. His clock was ticking and his palms were sweating. His fingers rubbed together anticipating the soft feel of new money.

"Hey man, the cash is in here, I've just got to dig around a little," said the voice from the room.

Steven knew the man from earlier sales, but the woman in the kitchen was new. She swayed at the entry with both of her hands raised to her mouth. Steven tried to ignore her, but he knew she was just some broken women turned into a dirty whore. Why did they always have to come in pairs? There was always some thin guy who ran the show and some woman hanging around like cobwebs. She was trash and he wanted her out of his mind. She was chewing her fingernail with a reckless abandon, moaning to the crunching rhythm. She was thin, too thin. Her clothes hung loosely on her bony shoulders and he could see the sores on the legs and arms. Wounds picked, dried and picked again. Her hair draped across her face and into her eyes. He could hear her sniffing as she chewed and chewed.

Her voice was raspy, "What you lookin' at hon?"

Steven glanced at her vacant face, "Nothing, just waiting here."

She slowly ran her hand over her chest, squeezed her empty breast, before continuing down into her shorts.

He could see her hand pulsing, "You like what you see?"

Steven felt sick at the sight, "No, I'll pass."

She smiled, "You don't know what you're missing out on." Steven did. He had sold to women like her before. Part of giving up on trades included these types of women. Mainly he feared getting something that antibiotics couldn't cure.

"No trades tonight." Steven called into the empty room, "Are you almost done? I have a few more errands to run tonight. A couple more buyers to see."

He could hear the man ruffling through papers and boxes, "You're a busy man. I understand. Just another minute. I almost got it."

A noise caught his attention and Steven turned his head to the right. Was it another voice? It was faint and distant, almost like a cry.

"You guys are the only ones here? I thought I heard someone else"

The man's head lifted up, "Yes, it's just us. Might be one of the neighbors. They make a lot of noises. No issues, I almost have it here."

The woman shifted in the kitchen. She stood half hiding behind the wall. He could see only half her face, just one eye peering from behind the molding and sheetrock. Steven felt nervous and a sickness was rising up in his stomach.

The sound came again. Was it just his mind moving through the end of his earlier hit? He swore he heard something, something distant. He thought, *was there a baby in this house?* He listened again, this time keeping the woman in his view. He narrowed his eyes and strained to listen. Nothing. He was startled out of his focus.

"All right. I found it. It's in here. Can't be too safe these days." Steven walked into the room to see the man holding a locked tin. Using a small key he opened the box to reveal a fold of cash.

"Do you have it all?"

"It was, was it 250? Do you have change for 300?"

Steven reached into his pocket, "Yeah I got a 50."

Steven was too focused on the deal to hear the girl move behind him. She glided through the doorway and raised her arms up. By the time Steven saw the shadow in the man's eyes, she had lowered the bat across his head. Steven fell to the ground with his arms outstretched. The small wad of cash fell out onto the floor. Steven sprawled out onto strewn newspapers, knocking a tray of needles to the floor. Steven didn't move as his jacket flipped over his head. The man scrambled and picked up the cash. He hovered above, moving his hands quickly along his body into his pants pockets. He checked his socks and shoes looking for more cash. He grabbed the bags of ice and cash and pressed them into his torn gray sweatpants. He leaned over and began to pull on Steven's leg with his butt in the air revealing his shit stains to the light.

"Fuckin' do me a favor and grab his other leg." The bat fell to the ground and the woman reached for his foot and began to pull.

They both strained to move him. The woman was breathing heavily with her back arched to the ceiling, "How much did you get?"

"Couple hundred and some bags."

"Ice?"

"Yep." He heaved and pulled. They dragged Steven across the floor as his face ground in the dirt and carpet. Loose needles caught on his jacket as he passed over garbage, dirty plates, and soiled newspapers. They entered the kitchen and laid him near the wall, next to the table that was piled high with clothes and pots.

"Go get the plastic wrap." The girl crossed the kitchen and began to open drawers pulling items out onto the floor. She spun around holding the plastic wrap up in the air. Steven began to stir on the floor, his legs softly moving as he uttered groans searching for consciousness.

"Hurry, hurry! I think he's starting to wake up."

The man lifted Steven to a sitting position and sat down behind him pulling both arms back. Steven's face was exposed to the kitchen. He let out a sigh and his eyes began to open. He could begin to hear the voices in the room. His mind fought to bring him back to reality and to warn him of the danger.

"Quick, pull out the plastic," he cried to the woman. "Now wrap his face!"

"I don't know...I don't know if we should do this," the woman nervously said.

"You better put that plastic on or you'll be next." The man's eyes were wide and spit flowed down his lips.

She knelt down and began to wrap Steven's face in the plastic. He slowly resisted, feeling the foreign material on his face.

"Wrap it tight. This boy's going for a ride." The man's knees dug into Steven's back stretching his arms and opening his chest. The woman lowered herself pressing the plastic into his face. Steven took a breath and felt only resistance as the plastic formed a hold over his face. His body tried to pull again and again but to no effect. Panic set in and messages fired from body to brain and back again. His eyes opened for the first time. Through the plastic, he could see the cloudy face of the woman struggling and contorted in the light, gaps in her mouth where teeth should be. There was a tightness in his chest as his arms wrenched back, feeling as if they might break loose and float away. Bony knees pressed on his spine sending pain running down his back and through his legs. He began to choke as his body strained and his lungs heaved.

Panic set in and Steven began to kick wildly towards the woman. He connected with a kick to the stomach and she crumpled to the floor. The pressure on his face relaxed and through the weave of plastic, he pulled a small draft of air. It was enough to subside the need for oxygen. He gathered his strength and pulled his head forward. The man behind Steven fought against this new found strength as Steven launched his head back and connected on the bridge of the man's nose. Blood began to pour out across his face. He lost his grip on Steven and brought his hands to his face, cupping his nose. Blood poured through his fingers and each breath sent droplets out sprinkling the floor.

In one motion, Steven leaned forward removing the plastic and stood in the kitchen. Where moments before he was lying helpless at their mercy, he now reached into his pocket flipped the safety and pulled out his gun. He swung to the man whose eyes met the barrel. There was no pause in his mind. Steven's focus was survival and he wasn't about to let two drugged out skeletons take that from him. He didn't think about the future or the law or the lives of these people. Steven cocked his head as he pulled the trigger. The bullet ripped through the man's face releasing blood and matter onto the wall behind him. Steven turned to the woman who put her hands up to him in an effort to block steel with flesh and bone. He released the slug and took the woman's right index finger off before grazing her right temple. Two more pulls of the trigger silenced her screams. He stood in the room, smoke flowing from the bodies and the strong smell of powder in the nose. His face was shadowed by the light and dark lesions of wet blood dripping down his cheek. A silence flowed over the room as life left the two quivering bodies.

Deep within Steven's mind reality bubbled over. *You need to move*. Steven stood there breathing heavily still shocked at what just happened. *You need to move*. He released another breath. *Move!*

Steven dropped to the floor and pulled the cash from the man's pants. The extra 250 dollars the man flashed was two twenties and a wad of ones. His need for money caused him to break his rules; he had walked into a trap. He knew never to let anyone get behind him in a deal. Steven collected the cash and bags. He pulled a cloth rag from the table and retraced his steps. He began to wipe down the railing and TV edge. He walked to the living room entry and ran the cloth over the entire molding. A quick look back and he opened the door wiping the knobs on both inside and out.

The widowed woman in unit 335 had muted her rerun of Jeopardy. Alex Trebek's face was paused on the screen ready to correct the contestant's wrong answer. She was leaned over her couch with her thumb separating the blinds of her main window. She looked out and watched Steven carefully wipe down the door entry and railing with the rag. She had heard the yelling and noise and turned up the volume, but the gunshots proved a different distraction. She watched Steven cross the green lawn and walk down the street, he got into his car and sped off into the night. She reached for the phone.

The ringer buzzed against her ear. "911, what is your emergency?"

"I would like to report a shooting."

CHAPTER FIVE

Officer Conners walked up to the townhouse. Red and blue lights flashed behind him and cruiser headlights lit up the driveway illuminating the path to the front door. He approached an officer standing on the porch vigorously writing in his notepad.

"How long ago was the shooting?"

The cop looked up. "Evening, officer. It was called in 20 minutes ago by a neighbor who said she heard some yelling and then gunshots."

Conners looked over the officer's shoulder and through the entry. He saw the state of the house. "Looks like a possible drug deal."

"We found some weed and meth in the kitchen. Lots of pipes and a hazmat level of needles in the rooms. We are assuming right now it was some type of deal gone bad." Officers walked out of the front entry, their hands gloved in latex and blood.

"How many dead?"

"Two bodies in the kitchen. One with multiple gunshots."

"If you don't mind, I am going to take a look around."

The officer pointed with his pen. "Not a problem. The bodies are in the kitchen. Do you need gloves?"

Conners shook his head as he rolled the gloves onto his hands. He walked up the porch and into the entryway. It was like a broken dam as he smelled the decay vigorously pouring out of the house. He rubbed his heel in the carpet observing the dust and dirt spraying in his wake. Conners looked up to see two officers rounding the corner. One held a blanket to his chest.

"I need you to call CPS and let them know we've got an infant here that is going to need immediate care." He walked past Conners as the muffled whimpers floated by.

"Jesus," Conners whispered as he shook his head, wincing at the passing sight.

The officer from the porch stepped back into the room and tapped Conners on the shoulder. "We got an ID on the suspect's car, late model Honda Civic. Either black or dark blue."

Conners nodded and made his way into the living room and towards the lights and officers congregating in the kitchen. He stepped into the kitchen and observed the two bodies. On the cheap linoleum floor were scuff marks.

"Was there a struggle?"

"Yes sir, it looks like these two might have been pinning someone down, but ended up getting it in the end."

Conners kneeled down, his legs cracked and groaned with age. His hand ran over the heel marks, he could feel the grooves cut into the flooring. He thought to himself that whoever was here was kicking awfully hard to do this. His eyes drifted to the plastic crumpled on the ground near the woman. He picked it up and carefully unfolded it to its original shape. "Looks like they were trying to strangle someone." Conners could see the outlines of a face in the plastic. His fingers gently touched the depression where Steven's mouth struggled for air.

He glanced over to the man slumped against the wall, his eyes staring at the far wall blankly into space. The blood had pooled around the bodies forming an irregular outline on the white floor. The officers quieted down and looked at Conners. "So from the shoe marks, it looks like we have a man, likely nearly died by plastic wrap, from these two meth heads. He got free from them, shot both of them and is now somewhere in a twenty mile radius of here in a dark colored Honda Civic. Have we put out a notice to patrols in the area?"

"Yes, sir. We sent the notice out moments ago."

"I think we understand motive here. We need to know if there was anyone else in the house when this happened, other than the innocence that was carried out of here a few minutes ago."

"The neighbor says she only saw the one white male leave."

"Looks like these guys didn't want to pay. I don't care what the circumstances are, I want this guy brought in tonight. He's already shot two which tells me he is either out of control or desperate."

CHAPTER SIX

The bar counter had a smooth wood finish with grooves and worn creases from elbows and glasses. The finish was faded around the falling lip, pointing to the red-topped swivel chairs lining the counter along one side of the narrow room. Dart boards were occupied by focused drunks. Holes and loose darts lodged in the wall proved their skill. Large flat screens that flickered with athletes held a grip on the patron's eyes.

Behind the counter, Jennifer worked to maintain the drink levels. Rows of bottles hung along the wall bathed in orange accent lighting. Her hair was pulled back in a ponytail and the blue and green ribbon told the attendees it was football season. Her hands washed beer glasses in the sink. Her eyes drifted up to the man staring down at the empty glass, "Honey, you want another, Jack?"

The man arched his back, sucked in his lips, and let out a hiss, "It's early and a Friday and I spent the day putting bolt assemblies on fuselages, so I think I will."

Jen smiled pulling a fresh glass from under the counter and swinging the bottle. She turned and the brown liquid fell out into the glass. She winked, "A little extra for your hard work today."

The man leaned back, pulled out his wallet, and dropped down a five, "That is all yours." His arms curled around the glass and he raised it up and sipped.

"Thank you, hon." She pulled the five and placed it into the register pulling out two ones and placing them into the tip jar. "I've had a long one too."

"Oh yeah, I'm sure this place was filled with the early shifters. They are grinding on us right now. Always wanting more planes pushed out the back."

"I hear you. This is my second job. Worked the coffee hut this morning on the south side and I finish the day here at the bar. The end of the day, you can just feel it. I think I've served almost a thousand drinks today. Drink after drink after drink."

He lifted his glass to Jennifer, "Cheers to you. I thank you for my drink. You power the city in the morning and calm us in the evening."

The door opened and a figure walked in from the cold night. His shoulders were slack and his eyes were dark and empty. Shaking off the rain from his shoulders he let his jacket open up to the warmth. Steven walked up to the edge of the bar on the short side and sat down. Jennifer turned her head and began to walk down the length of the bar away from the noise.

"Hey sweetie, you look like you need a drink."

Steven smirked, "You don't know the half of it."

"Long day I know. What do you need?"

"Another day."

Jen smiled, "I've got top shelf, locals, imports, but no time. Sorry honey."

Steven was resigned that she would not grant him his wish, "I could go for a tall Manny's right now."

"Alright, the 16 coming up." She reached out grabbing the small dusty bowl. "I'll get you a fresh bowl of pretzels too."

"Thanks," his voice trailed off. He leaned and pulled out his fold of bills. She returned with the amber drink and dropped down a precarious tower of salty pretzels.

"Do you have change for a hundred?" He held out the bill with two fingers. He was distracted and missed the bloodstain across the 1's and 0's.

"Oh, I'll check the register." Jen walked down the bar and Steven's eyes followed behind watching the sway of her hips. She opened the register and thumbed a short stack of bills. She returned, "I'm sorry sweetie, that would clean me out. I have an ATM in the back."

Steven nodded and got up crossing the bar. He approached the small machine, removed his card, and followed the instructions on the screen. Steven could see the blood-stained freckles on his fingernails and jacket cuff. He'd spent the last half hour furiously rubbing the blood from his hands and face, but he must have missed some. The machine whirred to life and spit out the last of the money in his account. He walked back and placed the twenty on the counter.

"Thanks honey. Sorry about that. We're just not allowed to keep that much cash in the till."

"No issues."

Jen walked back to get the change. Steven looked down at the glass, lifted it, and took a long pull. The beer left cascading rings of foam down the glass side. He stared at his right hand rubbing his thumb and studying a blood fleck in the wrinkle of his forefinger. A small faded soot mark was still visible in the webbing of his hand. His eyes drifted. He could feel a tightness in his chest and a pulling sensation from his lungs. His legs kicked slightly in the chair and he quivered. He took another drink trying to relax his nerves. He shuddered at the echoes of the shots in his mind. He could still see the smoke lifting from the man's face and the blood pooling around his back and arms. He saw the tremor in the foot as the life passed. Steven was lost in his mind and did not see Jennifer bring his change back. He came out of his dream to see money sitting next to his drink. She had left and was talking to a drunk at the end of the bar.

"Shit always sucks, trust me, I know." An old man three seats down from him was staring across the bar to the wall.

"I'm sorry?"

"Distractions, man. That is what separates what you have and what you need."

Steven looked around and then up to the wall, "Are you talking to me?"

"You're the only one here, right?" The man turned his gaze to Steven.

"What are you talking about? Distractions? "

"You look distracted so I'm asking what that distraction is. Lemme guess, the usual, women... your job? Or my personal favorite, money. It's always about the money in your mind. Everything reduces to that. Right there on that bar table. Just when you think you got it you need to be bailed out by the lotto again."

"Ok." Steven tried to ignore the old man's ravings. He took another sip of his drink.

"It's always the lotto, that's the key. Just get a ticket and boom! Beach and sun." The man smiled down into his drink. "You going to win me that lotto?"

"I could go for a lotto ticket. I don't even mind winning. Tenth place would be just fine." Steven drank.

"You're young, man. What I would give to know then what I know now! Oh, what I would tell my dumbass self 30 years ago. I'm not talking about that whole time traveling thing. Goin' back in time talking to myself. I talk to myself enough to know my younger self would've just kicked my ass. I would need something more subtle. Hell, I'd take a sticky note telling me to *Watch yo ass boy, love me.*"

"A sticky note? How would the younger you know that the sticky note would be from your future self?"

"It's not about analyzing the note or knowing who it's from. It's where the note would be placed, time and place. I only need to see it once and maybe things will turn out differently. It's like a lotto ticket. It's a loser most of the time but the right time and place, it is a winner."

"Alright man, if you think it would be that easy. Just put a sticky note on the fridge?"

"Yeah man I can see it, I would slip into the house. My dumbass drunk self wouldn't know I came in. I would place that sticky note right here on my forehead. I would wake up, walk into the bathroom, and see my future self's sagely wisdom cross my forehead and I would know." He snapped his fingers catching the edge of his glass. The beer sloshed as he fumbled catching the glass before it spilled.

"So that is your wisdom, *Watch your ass*?"

"Time and place, my friend." The man pointed at Steven. "It's all about the context. You do it any other time and it means nothing. But at that moment, it is like a punch in the gut."

The old man stood up and leaned back stretching. He pulled the beer up to his mouth and finished the last drops. He put his jacket on and started slowly limping to the front door. From the other side of the bar, Jennifer called out, "Have a good walk home, Harold." He waved blindly and left.

Steven could feel a buzz in his pocket. He reached down and pulled his phone out. *Juan. Tick Tock, my friend.* Steven's hand shook pulling the beer to his lips.

He swiped into his phone and selected the open message with this brother.

You need to get out of the house. The message moved from delivered to read.

Ok. I'm leaving now. Should I tell mom?

No. Just go.

Ok. What's going on?

I'll tell you tomorrow.

Fine. I'm leaving.

His mind raced through the day, pawn stores, begging friends for money, dealing the last of his product, gunshots, and the blood. He could feel a sickness welling up in him. His stomach felt the knots. He was losing control.

Steven looked up and found the sign at the back of the bar. He shot up and quickly walked down to the bathroom. He dipped his head into the sink. Water splashed on his face dripping off into the cracked white porcelain. He looked in the mirror and saw his face for the first time that day. He looked old. Eyes worn and cheeks sagging. There were blood veins wandering in the whites of his eyes. His pupils were dilated. Drops of blood still on the edge of his hairline. He wetted a paper towel in the sink and began to rub, the red drops running down his face. He rubbed again. He could feel the hourglass leaving behind the last of the grains.

There was a pulse in his stomach, he turned and fell to the stall. Dirt and matter collected around the edge of the bowl. He heaved and let loose the beer. His mouth open and eyes wide. He stood slowly from the stall dusting off his pants and kicking the stall flush. The splashing of water brought him back to the moment. He could hear the bar outside the door, people cheering loudly. He placed his hands onto the sink and bowed his head seeking guidance. His eyes released tears onto his cheek and his voice cracked, "Please get me out of this."

Outside the bathroom door, a man yelled, "You said you would take me on your trip! Just think about it; Alaska, glaciers, with this body carved out of granite."

"You wouldn't be able to keep up and granite is not built with beer."

"You just give me a chance Jenny, I'd show you the world," the words slurred.

"Just put some money in the fund and I'll pour you another drink. That's about all you're going to get, sweetie."

"Alright, here's a few more for you."

"Look at that everyone, I've even melted the coldest heart. All I know is that I'm going to sleep well, eat well, and have someone else serve me drinks."

Cheers, whistles, and claps came through the door. Steven's head was turned to the voices and sound.

"Aw, you deserve it, sweetie," a soft voice said.

"And that lovely voice means my evening is through. The beautiful Amy here will close you guys out. Thank you."

Steven stood up and wiped the remaining water from his face. He gave himself a look in the mirror. He was resolved to take action, this was his message. He opened the door and walked out into the noise. He crossed the length of the room, grabbed the change off the counter and left into the night.

CHAPTER SEVEN

Jennifer exited the bar stepping out into the orange glow of the street lighting. The clouds had cleared briefly revealing the stars above. The temperature had dropped and she shivered, pulling her rain jacket close to her lips. She let out a deep breath, a cloud emerging from her lips disappearing into the night's air. She reached into her pocket for her keys. From down the street, she heard the sounds of cars honking and in the distance the freeway in the death throes of the evening commute. A breeze picked up and the tall cottonwoods shielding one hundred year old homes began to sway under its force.

She rounded the corner of the bar and followed the line of parked cars. She opened the door and fell into the old seats. The car came to life and she lowered the seat belt into the connection. She looked up at the stereo which read, *no connection*. She looked around the car and finally felt her jacket pocket.

"Shit," she muttered. Jennifer turned off the car and quickly retraced her steps back into the bar. The quiet evening gave way to the bar's bustle and lights.

"Back so soon?" said Amy.

"Yeah, I just left my phone under the counter." She opened the cabinet and pulled out the phone, putting it into her jacket pocket. "You ok for the night?"

"No worries here, I've got these amateurs," Amy smiled.

She patted Amy on the butt, "Don't let them run all over you." Jennifer looked at the men in the front row and pointed to them, "I'm talking about you, yay-hoos."

They hollered as Jennifer exited the bar. She rounded the corner and opened the car door. Her radio came to life as she pulled away down the street and onto Broadway. Another turn and she merged onto the highway heading west towards Lake Stevens.

Her music faded and a ringing came across the speakers. She leaned over and pressed the accept button.

"Hello," she said into the void.

"Hey, sunshine."

"Hi grandma, how are you?"

"I was just checking to see if you were off work and heading home. "

"Yes ma'am, I am. Thank you for checking. I've just got to run to the bank to deposit tips from the night and swing by the store. Do you need anything?"

"No sweetie, I'm fine, but thank you. How was the take tonight?"

"It went well."

"Any issues?"

"Just a pile of harmless drunks and the neighborhood regulars."

"That's good. You working at that bar always make me nervous, but I'm happy you're heading home." Her grandmother owned conversations often switching subjects at will, "I was on the television and was flipping channels. I was between my shows. Did you know that Survivor show is still on? The people were running around naked, can you believe it? Now they had everything shaded out, but those poor people were out there with no sunblock. I can't imagine the burns." Jennifer was smiling as the voice rolled over the speakers.

She leaned back in her seat enjoying that her day was through and that she would soon crawl into bed and sleep. "That sounds really interesting, grandma. Now I'm getting into town. Did you watch Judge Judy yet?"

"Oh my goodness, I couldn't help it, I watched without you. They was arguing over a dog cleaning bill. They had the cutest dog, it reminded me of Remmy, my old dog. You remember Remmy? You were real young at that time but boy was that dog smart."

"Yes, I do remember Remmy…" She was cut off as her grandma continued.

"This dog was cute as a button too and did tricks for the judge. I think it was one of them puggies or something like that. Real small dog."

Jennifer smiled, "Grandma, I'm going to let you go. I'll see you in a little while. "

"Ok, I've got the cop show here if you want to watch."

"I'll see about what time I get home, but sure. I've got tomorrow off and I can stay up a little tonight. Save me some of that pie from last night."

"Alright, I haven't had any."

"Somehow I don't believe you. Love you."

"See you soon. Love you." Jennifer could hear Judge Judy's voice in the background as she ended the call. The music returned to the car as she merged off Highway 2 and onto the 204.

From behind Jennifer, Steven's head appeared. He rose up in complete silence taking over the backseat and settling behind her head, sitting perfectly upright and still. The reflection of oncoming traffic lights illuminated the car reflecting off his dark body in the backseat, his eyes stared blankly into the back of her head. Fabric covered his mouth and nose as his chest rhythmically moved up and down.

Jennifer continued down the empty road and caught the green light merging onto Highway 9 heading south. Steven sat outside her vision. He glanced through the windows behind and around the car. The road was empty and the light ahead flipped from green to yellow, and eventually to red. Jennifer slowed the car to a stop as the music continued to play masking Steven's movements behind her.

Steven's left arm lifted up and grabbed the side of her seat. His right hand lifted and the glint of light reflected off the gun barrel. He moved slowly and pressed the lock on the driver side door. The entire car responded and locked the remaining doors. The sudden action by the car jolted Jennifer as she quickly looked to her left just missing the retracting hand. The figure shifted and reached forward pulling the car into neutral. She heard the clicking of the shifter and she saw Steven's arm retreating behind her. She turned to see a set of eyes looking down at her. Panic and fear began to swell inside of Jennifer as she stared at Steven's face.

Steven grabbed her mouth muffling a scream and pressed the gun against her head. She reached out and grabbed the steering wheel and smashed the gas pedal. The car roared to life but did not move. She pressed the gas again and again and still no movement.

"Take your foot off the gas," Steven yelled. She could feel the heat of his breath on her forehead as the gun dug into her skull. She let out a muffled scream that ended in a long cry as the tears fell into the kidnapper's hand.

"I'm not going to hurt you, but I need you to cooperate." Jennifer's chest fluttered as she continued to sob. "I want you to follow my orders, but you need to listen to me."

The light turned green. Steven could see from the reflection in the rearview mirror that cars were cresting over the hill and they needed to move fast. Jennifer's eyes stared at Steven's, but she continued to cry.

"You need to drive this car to your bank, you need to do that now or I will be forced to dump your body on the side of the road." She could barely register what was happening to her. How did he get into the car,? she thought. He leaned in, "Do you understand me?"

She sobbed but nodded.

"I'm going to put the car into drive and I want you to take me to the bank." He pressed the gun to her head and shifted into drive. "Now go."

He lifted his hand from her mouth, "Please let me go, please." She could barely speak through her tears and panicked breathing.

"Drive." Steven's voice boomed in the small car.

She cried out and looked around assessing her situation as if it were the first time she stepped into a car. From behind, vehicle lights approached and a car passed on her left. A car slowed behind them and honked its horn before swerving into the next lane and continuing on.

She lifted her foot from the brake and the car began to roll. "What do you want from me?"

"Just go to the bank." The gun continued to press against her head. She looked in the mirror to try and identify the man in the back. She saw the cloth around the face and his eyes scanning ahead and to the side.

"Which bank am I going to?"

"Your bank." He turned his head slightly like a dog and she could see his cheeks rise up. She knew he was smiling.

"What do you want? Why my bank?"

"Just shut up and drive." She pulled away from the light and continued down the road.

CHAPTER EIGHT

The shopping center was empty save a few cars cozied up outside the corner bar. The lights from the bar flooded the parking lot and a soft drum of muffled music could be heard. The car sat idling in a parking space pointed at the bank with the lights off. Inside, two faces focused on the brick facade as the gun pressed into Jennifer's neck. The blue light of the bank sign fell across her face. Her cheeks were wet with tears, melting mascara, and smeared lipstick. Her chin quivered in fear and her eyes were puffy and red and looked exhausted from the sudden change in her life.

"Reach down and hand me the tip money." She silently reached down and pulled up the cash between two fingers and passed it over her shoulder. Steven quietly thumbed the money with one hand. It was over one hundred dollars. He added the money to his jacket pocket.

"Listen to me. You're going to roll up to the drive-through ATM." He pointed over her shoulder. "I need you to take out 600 dollars from the bank."

"Please no," she muttered shaking her head.

He continued, "When you're done, I want you to drive behind the grocery store and park the car."

She began to cry again and her head was in her hands.

"You and I do not have time for this now. Move now, goddammit!" He pressed the gun to her neck. Jennifer released a short squeal and her hands weakly lifted trying to protect herself.

"I just want to go home. Please just let me go home."

"Listen to me, if you get me the money, I promise you this is over. You will get to go home and watch your shitty TV with whoever that was." Jennifer felt violated, a private moment with her grandmother had been spied on by this criminal. She had felt terrified up until now, but this made her angry.

"I think you're lying."

"Well you either do it or the lights will turn out forever." She wanted to get home but there was no easy way. She resigned herself to finishing this last task. She turned on the car lights, shifted into drive and pulled around to the ATM. Steven sunk down into the seat and pulled the gun back from her head.

"Stay calm. We will be in and out," His voice seemed to come from the bottom of the backseat. She knew that he was hiding from view. Jennifer looked at the machine and stared into the camera pointed directly at her face. She mouthed, *Help Me Please.* She inserted her card and followed the instructions. Steven could hear the machine come to life as the twenty dollar bills were pushed out. In his mind, he knew this was the last of the debt. There was a relief coming over him and for the first moment that night he felt that he may be able to get out of this alive. He felt some remorse about robbing this woman, but he was more concerned about surviving the evening.

Jennifer shifted into drive and drove through the parking lot. She was trying to get herself noticed and was failing to observe any driving lines. She carelessly rolled through stop signs exiting the center. She hoped that there might be some officer sitting quietly ready to make a quick $200 fine. She rounded the corner and parked behind the store.

"Pass the cash back."

She handed Steven the money. "Please let me go now, you've got what you want."

"I need you a little longer." He thumbed the money. "Get back onto the road and head north. I'll tell you when to turn."

"Please…you promised, you promised you would let me go." She began to cry.

Steven's arm moved and the gun fired. The car lit up for that fraction of a second. Two bodies could be seen clearly as Jennifer followed the gunshot with a deafening scream, her hands shaking next to her face. Steven's ears rang through the screams as smoke rose from the hole in the passenger seat. Steven shook his head and reached around Jennifer's neck to pull her back. He raised the gun to her temple. She was silent, tears streaming down her face, mouth open to the car roof.

He paused between his words, "Do you think this is a fucking joke?" She could see the whites of his eyes as they looked down on her, the vein pulsing above his eyebrow as he pulled back. She began to cough from the force on her neck. He let loose, "Slide over now."

She moved across to the passenger seat and sat in a fetal position curled towards the door. The intense smell of gun smoke ran up her shirt. Steven kept his hand on her shoulder as he slid into the front seat. His hand wrapped around her shirt and bra strap, stretching both and revealed red scratch marks and the white of her chest. He pulled his feet to the pedals. He put the gun down on to the ground and shifted from the seat back. He turned to Jennifer and pulled the seatbelt across her, shoving her back into the seat and clicking her secure. He reached with his left hand and shifted the car into drive.

He turned the car around and left the shopping center, entering the road and heading north as a light rain fell onto the glass. Jennifer had withdrawn in shock and remained curled up in the seat beside him.

"This is almost over. I've got an errand to run and it's over."

Jennifer showed no response to Steven. He looked across to her and removed his hand from her shoulder. She pulled it back feeling the release in an effort to distance herself from him.

Steven knew to let the situation calm down. It had gotten out of control and he regretted shooting in the car. He pulled away and drove down the dark highway. He crossed dark nameless hills with distant lights of large homesteads spotting the landscape. Tall evergreens dominated the dark night, wrapping the road, and hiding the evening sky. Steven's mind drifted as the oncoming cars passed him. Their lights drowning his vision. His mind left the car and focused on his goal, returning the money to Juan.

The side roads passed by as Steven eventually applied the brake illuminating the road behind him in a red glow. The car slowed and turned onto the gravel dirt road. Steven proceeded cautiously avoiding the carefully placed road holes. Each would swallow a car and were filled to the brim with rainwater. It was never easy to get there. Steven passed the dummy mailbox and turned down a side easement with a broken wooden gate. He came up to a small speaker box. Steven cranked on the handle lowering the window. He pressed the combination and a beep sounded.

"This is Steven, I need to speak with Juan. He is expecting me." There was a long pause. Steven took this time to pull the money from his jacket pocket. He collected the money into a single wad and placed the rubber band to form a roll. His eyes moved to the girl.

Her only movements were the rhythmic pulse of her chest as she breathed quietly. Steven shifted and pulled his jacket off. He carefully lowered it across the girl leaving only her head exposed. Jennifer pulled back quickly as the jacket rested on her shoulders.

To Steven's left a light went from red to green. The speaker cracked alive and a man with a thick accent said, "The pool house."

Steven knew that the pool house was not a luxurious beautiful white building with music, women, and fun. It was the junk area on the property, where junk was burned and the old oil drums would be stacked high. He had been there once before. He remembered being shocked by the scale of the junk site as Juan explained to him its meaning:

"Steven, this is the pool house." Juan looked at Steven with his arms around his shoulders. Steven held the shoebox full of bagged meth. "Do you see those drums? Those are fifty-five gallon pools." Juan smiled at him. Steven just stared forward. "I get them cheap, naturally, food-safe drums, I wouldn't want any issues with oil or other nasty things. In the long cool winters here in Washington sometimes a nice warm pool is the best. The best way to get them warm is to pull them up against a bonfire. Kind of like a redneck Jacuzzi," Juan's eyes remained focused on the barrel and he walked out ahead of Steven pointing to the welder, "It is important to make sure someone who is in the pool is secure. You wouldn't want an accident to happen so close to the fire." Juan turned petting the barrel, "To make sure that you get the true spa experience."

Steven shivered slightly and glanced at the clock, 10:50. He had made it just in time. Steven knew that Jennifer could hear his voice, "Stay still and don't move. These people won't help you. They might even make it worse. Just stay down and pretend to be passed out."

Jennifer's eyes opened and she peeked over her shoulder. She could see the red glow on the windshield ahead of her. The glow was dancing and she could smell a burning fire.

Steven rolled up to the edge of the pool house. The fire danced between piles of wooden pallets, old cars, and rows of oil drums. There was a metallic smell in the air that burned the nose. Silhouetted against the fire were four men. One man was poking the fire with a long rod and the other three turned to the headlights. Steven could see two shotguns leaned up against the welder. He pulled into a spot. The man with the rod turned and began to walk to the car.

He tapped the rod on the ground as he walked, "Steven, Steven, Steven." He glanced at his watch and smiled. "Good boy, just in time."

Steven reached down, pulled out the roll of money, and put his arm out. The man lifted the red-hot rod to Steven's arm. He could feel the heat and he pulled back slightly.

"Toss it here." Steven threw the money to the man.

"Juan, it's all there, man." The man thumbed the cash and placed it into his pocket.

"And just in time. I was starting to get excited for you." He looked into the car, past Steven, to the passenger seat. His voice lifted, "Who's this? You brought a friend?"

Steven looked to the passenger seat and then back to Juan. "Just a girl, man. She is nothing special."

"Nothing special, you say?" Juan's eyes ran down Jennifer's jeans and along her legs. "She looks special." His hand tugged up on his pants.

Steven tried to defuse the situation, "She's just wasted from earlier and I'm heading home." Jennifer's eyes were very wide as she hid her head beneath the jacket. She could hear the panic in Steven's voice. What had he gotten her into? Who were these men?

Juan's head turned smiling to the three men, "Chica del drogadicto."

Steven pressed, "Juan, I need to go. Am I settled? I paid up and on time"

"Oh yeah, you're paid up. I can imagine you have a busy evening with your girlfriend." His tongue flicked his teeth.

"I've got to go to a party tonight. Just have to head home first." The three men started walking towards the car.

"It's a long way home and there's a party going on here. You guys can stay."

Steven lowered his arm to the gear shifter and placed his foot above the brake.

"Steven," Juan rolled the cash in his hand and presented it back to him, "I'll give it to you for the girl. I'm sure you have to pay someone back for this." Steven paused and Jennifer's heart skipped a beat.

Steven considered the wager but knew that Juan would kill him just for knowing he had the girl. This was not a deal he should make. The men were nearing the front of the car. He could see their eyes focused on the girl curled up in the front seat.

The men were too close. He locked the car, shifted into reverse, and he smashed the gas. The wheels began to spin throwing rocks and dirt into the air. The three men ahead of him fell back with their arms protecting their faces from the flying debris. The car gained traction and began to roll backward away from the fire. He gained speed and flipped the wheel, turning the car as it slid along the gravel. He shifted the car into drive and pounded the gas. The car pulled back onto the easement. Steven's eyes focused on the road ahead of him as flashes lit up his rear view mirror. The first bullet flew over the roof of the car as the shot echoed through the trees. Jennifer screamed in fear pressing her head deep into the seat.

Steven yelled at her putting his arm on her head forcing it down, "Stay down." Another shot rang out and he could hear the bullet fly by the open window. He lowered his head and the car fishtailed on the gravel. He hit the gas to put distance between the flashes. Steven stared at the rearview mirror waiting for headlights to follow him down the road. He was breathing heavily and his hands were white from gripping the wheel. He hit the main easement and slid the backend of the car around the turn. The flashes stopped and he didn't see any lights following him as he sped away to the highway. He pulled onto Highway 9 and continued north.

Jennifer was sitting up now looking at Steven who was glued to the road and nervously gazing at the side mirror. Steven continued down the road for a couple of miles keeping his focus on any approaching lights. There were none. He relaxed and settled back into the seat.

Jennifer said, "Are they coming for us?"

"No. I don't think so."

"Are you sure? They were shooting at us."

"No. I think they were just trying to scare us." Steven knew this was a lie. He had heard the bullet scream by the window just inches from his head. He didn't want to imagine what would have happened if they were a better shot.

"Where are you taking me?"

"Work."

"Work?"

"They will know what to do because I'm fresh out of ideas. My mind is fried and Tyler will know what to do. I trust him."

Jennifer knew now what she had suspected all night, he was never going to let her go. She began to tear up again, leaning back against the headrest. She knew that she needed to get out of the car. She had to take a chance somewhere. She thought to herself if could she throw herself out of the car. Not at this speed, she would die rolling down the embankment.

Steven's hair whipped about in the open window as Jennifer's phone began to ring. He looked down to see *Grandma* on the screen. Jennifer's heart raced. This was her opportunity. She quickly moved to the phone and accepted the call. She screamed out, "Help!"

It was all she could muster before Steven took the phone and threw it out the window. It hit the ground along the grassy swale glowing softly as the car sped on.

"Stupid bitch!" Steven was furious and ground his hands into the wheel. He knew they would be looking for her now. This complicated things even more.

"You promised to let me go. Just pull over and I will get out. Just let me go," Jennifer cried.

Steven didn't answer. His anger was crowding out any clear judgment. He was focused on getting to work and having Tyler help solve this.

"She wanted to know where I am. I should be home by now." His face seethed with anger.

He pressed the gas and the car accelerated forward. The car sped on moving through the columns of tall pines. The road was empty as they crested over small hills. Dark driveway entrances dotted the side of the road.

Jennifer knew she needed to find a way to get out of this car. She looked around to see if there was anything that she could use. Steven's gun was tucked into his lap. Her phone was now miles behind them and there was a water bottle lying on the floor. The water bottle was hardly a weapon and she began regretting keeping her car so clean. Along the horizon, she could see the warm lights of Arlington. She knew that there were lights and roundabouts and that the car may slow down enough for her to jump.

She looked ahead and saw the soft lights accenting the "Welcome to Arlington" sign centered in the middle of the roundabout. The corner coffee hut was closed but the parking lights were still on. She turned her head softly to the right and saw the door lock. She was locked in, but she could quickly grab and unlock the door. She pretended to itch her right shoulder and leaned over to quietly unlock her door. She placed her right hand on her knee and eyed the door handle.

Steven pressed the brake as he entered the edge of the roundabout. There were no cars in the loop as he began to make the turn. They reached the right side of the loop and Jennifer could see the coffee hut. She reached over and pulled the door lever as she unbuckled the seat belt. The force of the turn threw the door open and Jennifer leaned out of the car. Her hands reached out and touched the road. The road scraped by and pulled on her jacket forcing her back to the rear of the car. She had an overwhelming feeling of falling. She tucked her head preparing for the impact on the road.

As she fell out of the car, a hand grasped her pants and held her back. Her legs began to kick wildly in an effort to break free from Steven's grasp. The force of catching Jennifer caused Steven to be pulled into the center console. His foot hit the gas and his hand locked the wheel as they continued to drive around the loop. They missed their exit as Steven locked his elbow and began to pull back. Jennifer, desperate to escape the vehicle, reached out for anything to grab. The door was completely ajar and began to smack the bushes that edged the roundabout. Jennifer grasped the leaves and branches leaving behind cuts and welts on her hands.

The car cleared the bushes and Jennifer screamed out for help with her last breath, a single hand holding her back from freedom. The car entered the loop again as Steven decelerated. He locked the wheel with his knees and pulled her belt loop with both hands. Jennifer's face was inches from the ground and began to return to the car door. Steven lunged back and hit his head against the door jam. Jennifer returned to the car. Her arms bleeding from the bushes and road rash.

She turned to Steven and began to strike at his shoulder and head. She connected twice as Steven exited the roundabout. He lifted his arm to block another shot as the door slammed shut. He smashed the brake and the car came to a stop in the gravel edging. Jennifer flew forward and hit her head against the windshield leaving behind a small crack. She fell back into her seat with a small trickle of blood running down her forehead. She laid in a crumpled mess in the seat, unmoving and still.

Steven turned to her in an effort to block more punches, but she didn't move. He relaxed and focused on her breathing. She was still alive. He quickly looked in his mirrors to see that the entire loop was empty. He was breathing heavily and took a moment to calm down.

Steven was shaking his head slightly as he tried to process what had just taken place. He reached over Jennifer and locked the door. He took the butt of his gun and slashed at the door shearing the lock off. He connected her seatbelt and continued down the road.

CHAPTER NINE

Officer Conners kneeled down in the street with his elbow resting on his thigh massaging his palm gently with this thumb. His eyes stared across the street to the profile of the navy Honda Civic. Blue and red flashing lights danced across the exterior of the bar and drifted into the night above. A misting rain returned falling in front of his eyes and graining his view. Yellow caution tape closed off both street entrances and police officers were moving about carrying vials of evidence between cars.

The sound of steps approached from behind Conners as he fixated on the scene before him. The beat officer spoke, "We ran the plates and they are reported to belong to a Steven Pfeffer. We've crossed that against the licensing department and we've got his driver's license image. We're passing that out to help identify him."

Conners stood brushing his hands on his pants, "Is this our suspect?"

"We are taking prints in the car and we'll cross them against what we find in the house."

"Did he leave anything in the car?"

The officer let out a deep breath. "We've checked the car over but have not found any sign of a gun. We did find drug paraphernalia, a pipe with residue in it. A couple of lighters. No money or drugs though."

"Do you think it's a dealer car? Do you think this boy might be involved in that?"

"It is possible. We found one hidden compartment under the driver seat, but no drop phones or baggies. We did find a new but opened container of hand wipes and paper towels. No blood on any of the packaging. We're bringing it all to the lab now to see if there might be something we can't see here at night."

"Any thoughts on him grabbing any evidence before he left?"

"Possibly. We're not sure when he left. Officers are walking through the local stores asking for anyone named Steven. A couple of squad cars are patrolling the area looking for any male on foot fitting his description."

"So the car is here." Pointing at the vehicle. His eyes looked up the street, "But where are you?"

"I don't think we'll find him accidentally walking up here. If he saw the lights he is probably laying low."

"That is a possibility, or he could be on the move again. My concern is that I've got a man who's killed two people walking around the streets armed and likely a little edgy."

The officers were lifting the yellow tape from the street and ushering the late night spectators aside. A loud beeping sound came from behind the group as the tow truck began maneuvering through the entrance. It rolled up lowering its rear gate behind the car.

The officer pointed at the truck. "We'll impound the car as evidence in the shooting."

Conners said, "Do we have a car going to the registration address?"

"We'll get someone on that."

"I want to know if he has been home tonight and where they think he might be going. Let me know if you find anything else." Conners began to drift towards the yellow tape. Sets of eyes beyond the barrier followed him as he approached. His hand jingled his keys in his pocket as he walked. He turned back to the officer he left behind and pointed to the street corner, "I'd check that bar. He might have gone in." He walked on around the corner to his unmarked vehicle.

CHAPTER TEN

Antonia stood on her porch with one hand pressed against the railing as she gazed down the quiet street. In the distance, a dog was rhythmically barking against the silent background. The screen door behind her was slightly ajar. The light was falling out onto the porch from the paused TV screen showing a face frozen mid-sentence staring at the empty chair. A cat moved across the opening, looking outside for a moment, before scurrying helplessly under the couch. She lived in a duplex at the end of a cul-de-sac surrounded by trucks, vans, and cars taking up residence along the street curb.

She hadn't heard from Jennifer and she was due home. The strain on her face showed as she squinted thinking about what might be happening with her granddaughter. Her eyes were hoping to see her car around the corner in the distance. She imagined the car pulling into the driveway. Her granddaughter would emerge holding a bag of groceries and talking about how her phone fell into a puddle at the store. She would hug Jennifer and tell her she wasn't worrying at all. She was only out on the porch getting fresh air.

Her hand trembled as she held the house phone. She felt this time her worries were justified, she knew something was wrong. She dialed her granddaughter and the phone rang repeatedly. She was about to hang up when the phone picked up. She knew this voice and it was in pain. The voice yelled, "Help!"

The phone went silent but the call did not hang up. She held it to her ear calling out to the cold night for her granddaughter. She screamed at the phone before she fell into a clump against the porch railing. Lights turned on in the neighboring duplex house and a young woman walked out of the door. "Antonia, is everything ok?"

Antonia was in tears as she sobbed with the phone in her hand. The woman came over and held her arms, pleading to know what was going on. Antonia recounted the call and returned to sobbing. The woman's eyes glistened. She was shocked that something like this could happen to Jennifer. She sprang to action pulling the phone out of Antonia's hand and dialing 911.

As the woman talked on the phone, Antonia continued staring off the porch down the empty street at the edge of the house on the corner. She stared hoping to see the house light up, but no headlights came.

CHAPTER ELEVEN

The rain had stopped to give way to a soundtrack of insects and frogs crying out into the night. Tyler and Kora stood next to Steven in the blue gravel driveway facing the car.

"What's wrong with you, man? Are you not thinking straight?" Tyler shook his head softly. Steven could feel the anger in his voice. He respected Tyler and hoped that he might be able to help. The sound of disappointment stuck in his mind. He had hoped that the pressure would lift once he was free of his debt, but now it was pouring down over his head threatening to drown him.

Tyler had been leading the prep teams for nearly a year when he pulled Steven out of dealing and gave him a job with his group. Tyler told Steven that if he wanted to survive, he would need to give up selling. It was a dangerous job and he was better suited on this side of the transaction. Like any job, there were some ups and downs, but even Steven would admit the risk of bodily harm was less. There was just one point that was stressed by everyone in the team, the job required a high level of trust. The trust was a requirement and a necessity. There are two rivers in this organization, the production river, and the money river. They would be entrusting Tyler and his team with a well of responsibility. The amount of product they produced on a weekly basis would lead weaker individuals to bad decisions. Every weekend the team would assemble in a new house and prepare for distribution. The organization picked up the cheap houses during the recession. They carefully distributed their purchases across the counties in order to limit suspicion. This weekend was like all the rest, the expectations, the same product and then go home.

They all stood staring at the passenger side window. Steven lifted his hand to his forehead rubbing hard and finishing through his hair. Sweat had begun to build on his brow as he let out a strained sigh. An undiscovered cut on his finger trickled blood down the back of his hand.

Kora looked to Steven, "Why did you bring her here? She's a liability."

Steven fought back, "She's 'out cold. She doesn't know where the house is."

"It doesn't matter. You're now tied to her. What are you going to do when the cops find out? When they ask what you do for a living? What are you going to tell them? Are you going to rat us all out?"

Tyler lifted his hand and Kora quieted down. They had been seeing each other for over a month, but when it came to work, he still controlled the floor. "I don't give a shit what your excuse is right now, Steven. You fucked up real bad. First, you mixed yourself up with Juan which is not good for your health in general and is in conflict with my boss. Second, you work for me and by that fact you also work for my boss. That means when you jeopardize my operation, you jeopardize his."

"I just needed help. I didn't know what to do."

Tyler was calm, "Again you chose to jump into quicksand and now you're asking me, Kora, and everyone else in this organization to jump in with you."

"What do you want me to do? Just drive away?"

Kora looked at Tyler, "He's still connected to her and he's connected to us."

"I understand," Tyler motioned to Kora. He looked at Steven, "Now, we've got to take care of this. We need to be able to trust you and this is a big breach of our trust."

Steven knew that he was in deep and he remained silent. Kora stood with her eyes piercing Steven's face. "You saw the pool house?"

"Yeah," Steven replied looking up at Kora.

Tyler turned his head, taking a deep and thoughtful breath. "Are you paid up with Juan?"

"Yeah. But he didn't like me leaving in a hurry." Steven looked at Tyler, "Dude, I know I messed up, but I need help. Just tell me what I should do."

Tyler lifted his hand and pointed at the white facade of the house, "I won't let this woman in this house. Do you hear me?" Steven nodded. "I can't make this decision. This is something my boss needs to know about. I am not about to jeopardize my job and my life for your mistakes."

The front door of the house was still open and the lights illuminating the kitchen showed tubing, trays, and materials stacked high on the table. Two other cars sat in the driveway alongside the group. Beyond the house were rows of dormant apple trees, overgrown green grass, and a small wooden house alongside the faded red pole barn. A small path was carved in the grass leading from one house to the other and a small well with a hand crank sat as a sentry to anyone passing by.

Tyler looked at Steven, "Are you emotionally attached to this woman?"

"What?" Steven shot back, surprised at the question.

Tyler's eyes narrowed and a deep breath signaled the seriousness of the response. His voice lifted to a yell, "Are you fucking her, you fuck?"

Steven recoiled and shook his head.

"No?" Tyler asked.

"No. I just met her tonight."

"I'm not trying to be an ass or splitting hairs, but you two didn't meet tonight. I wouldn't define it in the same vein as picking someone up at the bar after a beer and pleasant conversation." Steven lowered his eyes. "You kidnapped this woman. I don't give a fuck what you do in your personal life. You want to torture little doggies, get your rocks off with some meth whore, or be a fucking birthday clown because you have an untapped fetish. I don't give a fuck. I do give a fuck about your stupid ass rolling up in here, not in your fucking car might I add, with a woman who is bleeding from the head and sitting in the front seat. Not to forget we have a Mexican psychopath likely looking for you."

Steven took a breath to start but was cut off.

"You were supposed to come to work." Tyler pointed at the car, "This is not work. This is play time. Your play time. I'm going to ask you again and I want an answer. You obviously only meant for this to be a temporary thing, unless you were going to put her in your basement. Are you emotionally attached to her?"

"No, I am not," Steven lied. He felt remorse for the whole night and regretted it when he rode up to the house. From the first moment, Steven told Tyler the situation he knew he had screwed up. He never started the night thinking this is where he would end up. He never wanted this and know it felt like he was in more trouble.

There was a pause from Tyler, "Let me be clear once more, are you going to be upset if I shoot her in the head and scatter her body across the valley for coyotes to eat?"

Steven spoke quietly, "We don't need to do that."

"Now you step up and speak. Eh? You're going to tell me what I need to do when you take a shit on my driveway? We are working tonight. We are processing hash and making up balloons. I did not intend to have to deal with this, but now you're forcing me to. You don't get to dictate to me." Tyler closed the distance and finished inches from Steven's face. Steven pulled back as the closing words were shouted into his ear, "Do you understand that?"

From inside the car, Jennifer began to stir. Her legs shifted and she rolled over. She leaned back in the seat with her head looking up to the ceiling. She took a deep breath and raised her arm up over the welt on the top of her head. The semi-dried blood smeared across her forehead and left a streak on her arm and palm. Her eyes opened slightly looking through the window and across the driveway to the house. She began to take deeper breaths as she slowly regained consciousness.

Tyler calmly stated, "Steven, lock the car."

Steven looked up and saw Jennifer stirring in the front seat. He reached down and clicked the key. From inside the car, Jennifer could hear the doors lock. She turned quickly left and right but saw no one in the car. Movement pulled her eyes to the house as she saw a man quickly walking up to the front steps and stepping through the open the door. She turned and saw a man and woman staring down at her. Horror came across her face as she saw Steven and her memory flooded back. From the kidnapping to the shootout, to being dragged over the road. Her knees rose up, she lifted her arms, and she began to scream through the window. The sight of Steven was enough to unleash all of her anger and rage. She brought her hand down across the window, blood smearing on each strike and obscuring her vision. Jennifer heard the door from the house slam shut as an angry man crossed the gravel walkway. She saw the rag in his hand and a tin container. She continued to scream as her hand struck the window, "Let me out!"

From outside the car, she heard a muffled voice, "Unlock it."

At that moment she knew this man was coming for her. She scanned the car to look for a weapon. She saw the push lighter and pressed the button. The pop let her know the heating element as working. She began to crawl across the middle console to the driver side when the doors unlocked. The passenger side door opened as the man lunged into the car to grab her legs. Kora and Steven stood behind him unmoving as they watched the scene play out.

She kicked Tyler as he pulled her back. She grabbed for the door, but it was just out of reach. A click sounded and Jennifer grabbed the lighter and rammed it into Tyler's arm. He yelled in pain as she kicked again. She lunged and grabbed the door handle and pulled the latch. The driver side door swung open. She kicked again and connected on Tyler's shoulder. She lunged for the door, her head staring out the open door to the trees in the distance. She began to crawl across the seats with her arms reaching out for holds. She looked up only to see the face of Steven in the doorway. Their eyes met as Steven's hand grabbed the door and slammed it shut. She turned back to see Tyler pulling on her leg. As she looked back, Tyler smashed a rag into her face. She screamed and her breath gave out. She pulled another breath but her head fell limp. Tyler caught her and dragged her to the seat. He kneeled on the gravel and turned his head back to Kora. He took a deep breath, "Get me some rope. She is going in with the heads."

"The heads? I don't think she needs to go in there." Steven replied.

"Get me the rope, now."

They dragged her onto the grass and rolled her over onto her stomach. Her arms were pulled back and twine was wrapped around her wrists then slung together forming a bind. A piece of duct tape was pulled and placed across her mouth. Tyler reached into his pants and pulled out his knife, flipping the blade. He brought it close to her face and cut a short slit in the tape. They tied twine around her ankles and then bound both wrists and feet with additional duct tape. Steven and Tyler lifted her up onto their shoulders and carried her across the yard following the path that passed by the open well. They walked up the steps to the second house as Kora slid by and opened the door. They entered the dark house. Kora quickly scanned the nearest bedroom pushing papers and boxes around to check for bodies.

"All clear," she said.

They lowered her onto the old wooden floor as dust plumed up around her body. They slid her towards the open closet. From inside the room, you could hear the group leave the house, their muffled voices becoming more distant.

The room fell silent as Jennifer breathed quietly. The house creaked under the weight of slow-moving ghostly bodies. The soft moans and fingers scratching along the walls could be heard from the living room. Bodies lined up along the wall, slowly trying to escape from their nightmares. The moans gave way to occasional shrieks as a body would leap into the air, its head bobbing under its weight. Its eyes rolled back, sores lining its arms and legs, as its mouth hung open, teeth long gone. Steps would give way to stumbling causing the room to groan under the disruption.

Jennifer's body lay on the floor in peace.

CHAPTER TWELVE

Antonia called out from the kitchen, "Would you like any coffee? I have a pot left over."

Officer Conners looked up from the coffee table covered with tabloid magazines, "Yes ma'am, it's been a long day and I'd love a little."

"Cream and sugar?"

"Just cream, thank you." Antonia shakily reached up to her cabinet clinking the glasses. She pulled out the pot filling the cups carefully and adding cream to both. She walked around the corner and carefully set the cup onto the table brushing aside a magazine with her pinky finger.

"Sorry, the table is a little messy."

"That's not a problem." He smiled, took the cup, and sipped. It took all his effort not to show his displeasure. The coffee was old and burnt and no amount of cream could rescue it. He placed the cup down on the table and pulled out his notebook and pen. "Thank you, it's very tasty."

Antonia took a long drink from the cup and stared at the notebook, "She should be home by now. That voice on the phone. She sounded like she was in pain. It wasn't my Jennifer."

"I know. We'll work with you to get as much information as we can and we'll see where it takes us."

"I just want her home."

"The best thing to do is try and recreate where she might have gone."

"When I first called her she was on her way home from the bar."

"This is Jake's in north Everett?"

"Yeah, she's worked there for a while now, ever since she moved in with me. She'd just gotten out of a bad relationship. She left him and came up here to get away."

"This man that she used to live with, does she still talk to him?"

She shook her head, "No she promised never to talk to him again. She relapsed in the past, but he got violent which pushed her to leave and come home. He lives down in Portland, just east of the city. I think Jennifer said he is working at a salvage yard. I don't know if he's still there." The cup came her to mouth and she sipped again.

"Ok, so as far as you know this man hasn't come up to the Seattle area?"

"I haven't heard her talk about him in a long while so I would imagine he is still in the Portland area. His name is Ronald Trace. His friends call him RT for short. Sort of like the name Artie"

"Ok." Conners took down the notes, "You wouldn't happen to have a picture I could pass around?"

She walked to the end table and pulled out the drawer. She pushed aside papers and old photos, "I should really clean this place up." She ran through a number of photos before stopping and picking up a small photo, "Here he is."

She reached out and passed it to the officer, "Thank you, I assume that this is Jennifer in the image?" She nodded. "May I take this with me? I will return it."

"That's not a problem. You can probably keep it, I figure she doesn't care about images of him anymore. I'm actually surprised we still have one. He was a handsome man, but a real jerk. He never treated her right, in my opinion."

The officer smiled and tucked the image into the notebook. He looked up, "Do you know if this man drove a Honda sedan of any sort?"

"RT? No, no, that man wouldn't be caught dead with a car. He was a truck man, I remember that. He loved his trucks. Fords I think."

Conners nodded. "So after she left work she was heading where?"

"She told me she needed to run to the bank and do a couple of errands."

"Is it normal for her to do that after work?"

Antonia smiled and nodded, "She likes to put her tip money into the bank. She's had money problems in the past and it was her goal to start saving. If she had it on her, oh my, she would just spend it. You know how that is sometimes. She's been doing better about money now. She has been controlling her spending and I am real proud of her."

"So this is her tip money. Is that typically a lot of money?"

"Normally she earns a hundred dollars or so every day between the coffee hut and the bar. Its real good money if you don't have many bills or someone to take care of. She is staying here with me right now and I'm not charging her any rent."

"I understand." Conners wrote in his notebook.

"She had just saved up enough money to go on one of them Alaska cruises. You know the ones that take you out of Seattle and head up north?" Conners nodded. "She was going to go on one of them in a few months. She was so proud of herself for doing that."

Conners nodded as he continued to write.

Antonia began to tear up, "She's never been on that type of vacation before and she was so excited. At least once a week I would see her on the computer looking up pictures and seeing what was on the dinner menus." Her hand came up to her eye as Conners looked down and wrote in his notebook. "I'm just so happy she was getting the time to do this. She really earned it."

"Well, I hope she still gets to go on this trip," Conners tried to reassure her. "Something that could help us is knowing which bank she uses."

Antonia recovered from tearing up, "She uses a nice little credit union bank off the 9 here in Lake Stevens. I think it is called Northern Sound Credit Union. I think there is an ATM that is open all night that takes cash."

"Ok, so this is where we think she was heading after the bar?" Antonia nodded again, "We'll check with the bank to see if there might have been any activity during that time. There might even be some footage of her if she used the ATM. It will help us better pinpoint the timeline. We won't be able to get any additional information until the morning when the branch opens."

"Maybe there's some type of camera or something?"

"Exactly. Now, can you tell me about the phone call?"

"She was late. Later than I would expect. I just waited on my porch, hoping she would come rolling up. I gave up waiting and finally called her. The phone rang and rang and she eventually picked it up and yelled," Antonia's voice cracked. "She yelled 'Help' real loud. It sounded as if she was away from the phone. Like she was on speaker phone or something. There was a lot of noise before it went silent."

"Any idea what that noise might be?" Conners asked.

"It could have been road noise or wind noise. I think it did sound a lot like that, but a lot of wind. Maybe a window was rolled down in the car." Conners furiously scrawled in his notebook.

Conners leaned over and reached into his back pocket pulling out his leather-bound wallet. He opened the wallet and pulled out a thin white card. He turned the card over and wrote a series of numbers on the back and passed it forward. "On the back of the card is my cell phone number. If you hear anything from her, please let me know."

Antonia took the card and held it with both hands, "I will, thank you for your help."

Conners stood up and began to put his jacket on, "There was one more thing, do you know or has Jennifer ever mentioned a man by the name of Steven Pfeffer?"

Antonia looked down and her lips pursed to the side, "I don't think so, I haven't heard that name before."

"It would have been a white man, about five-ten, and in his mid-twenties, very thin."

"No, that name's not familiar. She doesn't tell me if she has a date or boyfriend or anything. You would think she would want me knowing about that. I'm her grandmother and I've got a right to know."

"Alright," Conners smiled. "We are going to try and locate her phone since it's still ringing. We will get back to you if we find anything."

Antonia nodded and Officer Conners opened the door walking out past the porch to his car. He got into the car and gave a light wave to the woman standing on the porch. He turned the car on and drove down the street rounding the corner. He pulled up on the side of the road and dialed a number on his cell phone. It rang in his ear, "Hello Officer Conners, what can I do you for?"

"I just got done talking to an old woman whose granddaughter didn't come home tonight. She thinks she heard her granddaughter scream for help on the phone."

"A kidnapping case?"

Conners' eyes drifted around the street. In the distance, he could see a man walking slowly up the sidewalk, "Yes, and the woman who is missing happens to work at Jake's. She was last heard on a cell phone call around the time our Honda was found."

"Related?"

"Possibly, we'll have to see, but according to her grandmother, she's never heard of Steven Pfeffer. The girl also has a recent nasty ex-boyfriend, but he is supposedly down in Portland."

"Do you think Steven might have hitched a ride?"

The man continued to walk up the sidewalk, his head down and feet shuffling. A ski cap was pulled down across his forehead and his eyes were fixed on the headlights, "The grandmother talked to Jennifer on her way home and she didn't sound stressed. Only the second call sounded worrisome."

"Alright, we're looking for possibly a man and a woman."

"I'll email in all of the notes and descriptions and we can push that out to the field." The man now passed the side of the car and bent slightly revealing the whites of his eyes to Conners. They stared at each other for a brief moment as he passed the window. Conners' hand moved to his waist and his fingers touched the butt of his gun. Conners followed the man in his rearview mirror as he continued on down the street.

"No problem, I'll wait for your email."

The phone call ended and Conners sat in his car. He closed his eyes. His mind drifted to Jake's where he could see a lovely young woman walking out of the bar and down the street to her car. His eyes opened and he shifted into drive and pulled off down the street.

CHAPTER THIRTEEN

The papers piled next to the cardboard boxes gently lifted as a draft moved through the room. Dust picked up into the air and swirled before crashing down to the floor again. Piles of trash, loose drywall, and insulation piled up in the center of the room. The clouds opened and the moonlight fell through the stained window onto the floor. The naked walls with exposed studs showed the home's age.

On the far side of the room, stretched out like a fallen dress, Jennifer's body slowly breathed. She lay quietly outside of the closet, her feet illuminated in the evening light. Her head rested on the floor as her arms were pulled back and bound at the wrists. Her legs were crossed with a foot dangling behind her calf. She was covered in a light dust as smoky plumes rose from her mouth on every breath.

Jennifer's shoulders began to sway and her goose-bumped arms folded and flexed under the binds. Her lip curled and cheeks raised as she slowly regained consciousness. Her eyelids danced and parted letting in the room. Her head shook brushing off the last of the chemicals as her eyes opened to the room tilted on its side. She slowly looked around as her memory warmed her to the situation. She lifted her head to listen and survey her surroundings. The bonds held strong fighting her weak attempts at freedom.

She rested a moment closing her eyes to the room and feeling across her body looking for any injuries. She squinted her eyes as her head rolled forward, the ground gently touching the welt on her forehead. Her body was sore but intact. She could feel the duct tape on her face as she tried to open her mouth, pushing forward with her tongue feeling the slit in the tape. She could taste glue mixed with blood from a wound. The knife had cut her upper lip and was draining across the tape. She pulled in a deep breath and let out a moan through the tape that drifted through the room.

Her head shifted as her eyes moved from the window to the door. She followed her body back and saw the open closet. Applying pressure from her legs, she rolled her shoulders and began to squirm her way to the closet. She touched the wall with her hands and pulled her knees in. It took her two pulls of the shoulder to lift her body against the wood on the wall. Two more pushes and she was upright looking out into the room. Her hands searched behind her as she felt the dust and rough wood.

Her head rolled from side to side assessing the state of the studs. She shifted slightly, hands guiding her movement, as she pressed her binds against the wood. She leaned forward and began to rock against the exposed stud, pressing hard against the edge of her binds. She could feel the heat from the friction, but the bindings did not give way.

She broke and took in long pulls of air. It was hard work in the contorted position and she couldn't get strong leverage. She leaned back against the wall to rest, closing her eyes, allowing her mind to focus on the distant noises. She held her breath and could make out scratching sounds against the wall and faint moans. Her eyes shot open when a loud scream came from the other side of the house. It was a guttural cry and finished with the thud of a body against the floor. It woke the house, as murmurs lifted, creating an ambient rhythm. Jennifer looked at the door and back to the window. She pressed her hands against the wood and began to furiously grind the binds. From the open slit in the tape, she muttered to herself, "Come on, come on."

She could feel the binding fray as pieces of material fell between her fingers. She wrenched forward, pulling her shoulders apart and pushing out at the elbows. The bindings did not give way as her hands went white from the strain. Her wrist folded over the bindings as her forearms turned beet red from stopped blood flow. She leaned back and the emotions began to swell. Tears slowly fell down her face and across the tape. Her chest popped lightly as she sobbed.

A scratch came from behind the door. Jennifer lifted her head to the noise. The room was silent, but a shadow could be seen shifting quietly. Jennifer's eyes opened wide as she realized she was not alone in the room. The shadow under the door shifted again and she could hear a faint panting. At the edge of the door, Jennifer could make out wisps of hair moving in the breeze. She wondered how long this person had been there. Was she being watched?

The hair gave way to a head that was looking down to the floor. Two hands crawled out in front as if searching for an unseen object. The man was on all fours and entering the room. His eyes were wide and wild, but unfocused. His head was trembling as if cold, and spit flowed from his open mouth onto the ground. His hands inched forward as his body emerged from the door. Jennifer pushed herself up against the wall trying to distance herself from the ghastly figure.

The man moved into the center of the room. His body was exposed except for dirty white briefs. Along his back and legs were sores and rashes. His skin was white and covered in dirt and dust. Boney knees left small trails of blood from open wounds as his crooked hands continued to crawl and pull him into the room. His body was impossibly thin with ribs and vertebrae jetting out. His white skin was pulled over his body like a loose sheet.

Jennifer was horrified. She thought, could this man even be real? Was she imagining this? Her stomach wretched and she held back a heave knowing that the tape would cause her to choke. She looked at his body and saw that his briefs protruded at his midsection. Her fear compounded as she realized he was erect. She moved slightly and her binds caught on the flooring. She pulled in a panic and tore part of the wood base up releasing a cracking sound.

The man stopped in the center of the room, quivering like a lone leaf lost in the breeze. Jennifer froze. He hadn't known she was here, but he did now. His head turned in an unnatural contorted manner. It slowly inched its way, squaring itself with the closet. Jennifer watched as his face came into view. Their eyes locked and for a moment she hoped that he might lose her in the shadows. His eyes widened and she knew he saw her. Her breathing increased and she started to assess if she could stand and hop out of the room. The man was not moving fast and probably could not stop her. She leaned her head forward and she pressed herself up against the wall. She could hear him turning and crawling towards her. She ignored the approaching horror and focused on her task. *Stand*, she told herself.

She could feel her back sliding up the wall, but she caught on a protruding nail and fell back to the floor. She tried again but failed. She shifted her weight to her side and popped herself to her knees. She lifted her body and pressed down trying to stand. She rose and stood on her feet, but her weight continued to shift and she overshot falling in a pile on the floor.

She turned her head, panting to see the man continuing to crawl slowly towards her. She saw his face as his arm reached out ahead of him. His legs moved in unison. Jennifer could smell his foul stench, a mixture of fecal matter and urine. His head was focused on Jennifer's face and she could see his briefs swinging under his chest. A slight smirk came across his face and she could see his yellow teeth and bleeding gums.

Jennifer looked around her but she could not find any object to use. She moved out of the closet and began to slide herself along the floor. The man was in pursuit. She shoved papers and boxes towards him as she moved to the corner of the closet. The man pushed aside the obstacles and began to crawl faster in anticipation of his catch.

Jennifer reached the wall and the man was only feet away. She turned to him and brought her knees to her chest to protect herself. The man lifted himself and fell on top of her. She could feel his cold flesh on her body. His chest rested against her shins and his arms touched her shoulder. His hands grazed her face and she wanted to vomit. She shifted her head to avoid his touch, each time squealing through the tape on her face. Jennifer pushed against the man with her legs and he fell back onto the floor. She brought her knees back as he gathered himself. Jennifer turned her hips and kicked at his face with her bound legs. She connected with her heal and sent him reeling to the floor. He let out a cry and clutched his nose. She could hear him gurgling on his spit. He shifted again and turned to Jennifer. She connected with her foot and the man dropped to the floor. Jennifer kicked again and she could hear the crunch of his skull under her boot.

She shifted in the closet corner and looked back on the sprawled body. Blood slowly poured from the man's face and she could see the small dent on the top of the head. The man's arms sat contorted and she could see the quivering of his fingers. Jennifer pulled her knees to her chest, arms still bound behind her, and she wept on her pant leg. Her mind was lost trying to search for meaning. Where was she and who was this person on the floor?

CHAPTER FOURTEEN

Steven followed behind Kora and Tyler on the walking path, his shoulders hung heavy as he plodded through the grass. They silently walked up the porch, opened up the door, and entered the house. They turned right into the large kitchen fanning out into familiar positions. They had worked this house many times before and they each had their favorite station. Laid across the countertops were packing supplies and small scales. Wash tubs with masking tape indicated sorted and finished material. Along the floor were two large trash bags giving off a sweet citrus smell. On the front, they were each labeled *Street* and *Medical*. The kitchen table contained a stack of brown cellophane-wrapped bricks of heroin each the size of a large textbook. A cardboard box sat next to the bricks and contained bags of clear methamphetamine.

"Kora, you're cutting tonight. The coke is on the table and the Leva and Benzo are on the floor." Kora circled around the kitchen island and picked up the industrial bag marked Levamisole and made her way to the counter. "Steven, you're on bud sorting and hash prep."

Steven looked at Tyler, "Are you kidding me?"

Tyler lightly bit his tongue, "Yes, you're bud sorting and hash, do you have a problem with that?"

"That's a shit job," he motioned to the bags.

"You're getting medicine duty tonight."

Steven stared down at the two trash sacks. His nose could smell the bags from the doorway. What he hated most was the after smell. There's no way to get it off your hands or clothes.

"I thought we were cooking tonight, man?"

"I did too, but we got the order to restock instead. I think we cook tomorrow." Tyler picked up the brick of heroin. His hand sagged under the weight.

"Steven, you can sort in a few minutes, but I need you on bag stamping first." Steven rolled his eyes and dropped his head. "The stamp and bags are in the box."

Steven walked over to the box and reached in. He pulled out a stamp rig, ink pad, and a box of wax paper baggies. The stamp was key for distinguishing their product from others. Customers knew the seal meant quality and repeatability.

Tyler walked across the room and pressed the power button on the speaker. The room quickly filled with music. Steven dabbed the stamp in the ink palette and pulled out a handful of wax bags. He set them up in a small stack alongside the rig.

"How many do we need?" Steven asked.

"I think this brick will give us a couple thousand."

Steven sighed and began to move. The stamp rig was wooden with a worn brass hand lever. Under the rig was a rubber mold perched above the stamping area. Steven grabbed a wax bag and placed it under the stamp and pulled down. He looked down and inspected the wax bag. The front was an image of a dragon and below was the word *Smaug*. He placed the new stamped bag on the counter. He repositioned his pile of wax bags and began to stamp. His hands moved in a methodical motion, grabbing a wax paper bag, moving it into place, and pulling down on the stamp. He then moved that new bag into a pile and continued. Every tenth bag he would re-apply ink by pulling on a small lever revealing the ink pad beneath the stamping area.

Steven broke the silence, "Why do we need to work here next to that house of horrors?"

Tyler responded, "We're here because we were ordered to. I think the other houses are occupied this weekend and this one was free."

"I just wish we could be at that house from last week."

Kora jumped in, "I always enjoyed that one. The pool and the pull-out couch." Tyler and Kora shared a brief glance before continuing.

Steven turned around and pointed to the two of them, "Exactly, I'm just saying the last time we were here one of them wandered out onto the lawn. I nearly shat myself walking to the car to smoke and running into a skeleton in a gown."

"It's not our job to question where we work. We just do our job and finish on time. They trust us in these homes and we can't screw that up." Tyler's voice silenced the two.

Steven was making good progress as Tyler parted up the brick of heroin into a gallon Ziploc bag and combined it with an entire container of powdered calcium.

Steven looked at Tyler and smiled, "Calcium for strong bones. It's better than drinking your milk."

Tyler's mouth curled up slightly, "Honestly, it's a lot of calcium."

He zipped the bag and began to roll it in his hands working to incorporate the two powders. He opened the bag again and placed half a dozen spoonfuls of powdered sugar. He again resealed the bag and rolled it carefully in his hands.

Tyler reached over and pulled the small mountain of stamped wax paper bags from the side of the stamping rig. Steven never broke stride as his hands moved in rapid action. Tyler rolled the Ziploc bag down so that the powder was now at the top. He pulled out a small measuring spoon. With one hand holding the wax paper bag, he scooped and leveled the powder. He dropped the powder into the wax bag and closed the top in a single motion. He continued to fill each bag, building stacks of ten on the counter in front of him. When he reached five stacks he put the spoon down and bundled the stacks with a red rubber band. He tapped and leveled the bags before placing the stack into a small cardboard box. Tyler's job was to manage and everything he saw was money. He placed the bundle into the box and he thought to himself, *one grand*.

The music continued to be the only sound in the kitchen as the team methodically worked. Tyler felt a buzz in his pocket. He reached in and pulled out his cell phone to look at the message. *Call me*.

Tyler paused and then looked up at Steven, "I need to make a quick phone call. I'll be right back."

Steven narrowed his eyes, "Who is it?"

"It's the Boss."

Steven's eyes opened wide. He knew that this text message and call were about the girl in the house. He braced himself for what may come.

"Tyler, tell me if I am in trouble. I deserve to know," Steven said.

"Just let me make this call and I'll get back to you guys." Tyler walked into the living room. Tyler brought the phone to his ear as it rang.

There was a click and a voice on the other side, "We need to take care of this."

"I know."

"We have a guy. I'll text you his number."

"What do I do in the meantime?"

"Keep her in the house until the guy arrives." There was a click and the phone hung up on the other end. Tyler lowered the phone and waited for the message. His phone lit up with the message from his boss that included a phone number and a name, *Vadym*.

He texted back, *And Steven?*

A moment later, the response, *just call Vadym. I've already spoken to him.*

Tyler swiped the phone and clicked the number. The phone rang and continued to ring. He wondered if it would go to voicemail. He was ready to hang up when the ringing stopped and there was a voice on the other end. The man had a broken Russian accent.

The voice was deep, "Hello."

"Hello. Is this Vadym?"

"Da."

"I was told to call you to take care of a situation we have."

As if the man already knew the complete story, "How tall?"

"Excuse me?"

"How tall is the girl?"

"Five foot five maybe? She's not tall."

"Thin?"

"Yes."

"I've been told the man will help."

"Steven?"

"Yes. Text me your address to this number."

"How long will it take for you to get here?"

"I don't know. It depends if she fights me."

"No, I meant where are you located?"

"That's not your business."

Tyler was slightly confused, "I'm just trying to understand when you'll get here. We're east of Arlington in the mountains."

"I'll be there within the hour." The phone clicked. Tyler looked at the phone and texted the address to the number. A single message was returned, *K.*

Tyler returned to the kitchen. Kora and Steven were standing quietly in the center of the room. Tyler looked at Steven, "There is a man coming who will take care of the problem."

"What problem?" Tyler stared at Steven without saying a word. "Come on, man, we can't let that happen."

Tyler looked away and made his way back to the counter. "You're going to help him."

Steven felt sick, "Help him do what? Tyler, talk to me, what did the boss say? What is this about? I, I can't do that man. That's not me."

"Steven, this is out of your hands now. You will do what you're told. You have no choice in this matter." Tyler returned to the counter. "When is Nick getting here?"

"Tyler man, come on. We can't let something like that happen."

"When is Nick coming?"

Kora answered, "He should be here soon. I got a message from him a few minutes ago." She paused for a moment, "Tyler, what's going on? We can't hurt this woman. It's just not right."

Steven and Kora stood in the room staring at the back of Tyler's head. There were no answers to their questions. Tyler's voice was quiet as he turned his head slightly, "You guys need to forget about this and get back to work. It's out of our hands." He turned to Steven, "If you didn't want this to happen, then you should have thought twice about getting involved with Juan and then kidnapping this woman. Shut your face and get back to work."

CHAPTER FIFTEEN

Officer Conners stood on the street corner with his hands pressed against the small of his back. He gazed up the street where the navy Civic once stood. His eyes traced the path from where the car stood to the front door of the bar. Conners was flanked by two police officers holding notebooks in their hands.

"Shall we go in?" Conners asked.

"It's your show, boss," responded one officer.

Conners walked the sidewalk to the front door. The officers were bathed in the light from the neon orange *OPEN* sign that was mounted alongside the door. The street was quiet this late at night, but when the officers entered the bar they were greeted by TV screens and the remnant of a darts game. A lone drunk sat at the bar nursing the last of his whiskey.

Amy was behind the bar cleaning glasses from the night. She looked up to see the officers. She walked down the bar line to greet them, "Hello gentlemen, is there anything I can do for you?"

Conners answered, "I know some officers came by earlier this evening when we searched a car outside. We came back to ask some additional questions. Do you have the time to talk?"

"It's getting real slow here so I think I can help you out, no problem."

"So we were originally interested in the owner of that car that we found, but we are also interested in the woman who had the earlier shift, Jennifer?"

"Yes, she works the shift before me. Is she ok?"

"We don't know anything right now, but we're asking people who have seen her tonight."

"Wait, wait, is there something wrong with Jenny?"

"We just want to know if you knew where she might be heading this evening when she got off."

"Well, I think she usually heads over to the bank to deposit her tips from the night."

"That confirms what her grandmother said."

"I'm sorry, I'm not following. You seem to be talking like she didn't come home tonight."

"We were called by her grandmother when she didn't come in this evening. She placed a missing person's report and happened to mention the bar. The dispatch knew the bar from earlier in the evening and called me up."

"She didn't come home?" The bottom of Amy's eyes turned to a soft red color. She looked down as the first tear rolled down her cheek. Officer Conners pulled an unused napkin from the bar top and handed it to Amy. She took the napkin and blotted under her eyes so as not to run her mascara.

"As far as we know she is hasn't come home yet. I spoke with her grandmother a little while ago to hopefully find out where she might've gone."

"I don't know, we didn't talk about that. But I know she heads to the bank after work." Amy was fighting back more tears as she thought about Jennifer and what might be happening to her.

"Alright." Conners moved his hand through his hair as he thought about his next question.

"Do you think it might be related to the car you guys looked at?"

"That is an avenue we are looking at, but we're still unsure. Do you know anything about her old ex-boyfriend down in Portland?"

"She told me a little bit about him. All I know is that she described him as one super douchebag." One of the officers behind Conners smirked.

"Did Jennifer mention that she had been in contact with him recently?"

"No, not that I heard of and she would have told me," replied Amy.

"The cameras?" The officer to Conners' left said in a hushed tone.

"Oh yeah, you wouldn't happen to know how to use the security system that you guys have? We saw the cameras outside the entrance. One of those cameras is pointing at the corner and might've picked up something."

Amy nodded and motioned to the officers, "It's right here in the back." The three officers walked around the end of the bar and followed Amy around the corner. Behind the large wall of bottled alcohol was a tiny office. The office was sparse but for the table and chairs and a wall of documents and binders. On the back wall was the framed liquor license for the bar alongside the business license. Amy walked over to one wall where the monitor displayed a series of images from inside and outside the bar.

Amy pulled the keyboard out and used a mouse to navigate the screen. She typed in a password and a couple of clicks later, she turned to the officer, "When do you want me to go back to?"

"Can we go back to when you came on shift? Specifically the camera outside."

Amy made a number of selections and the screen displayed the camera view. It showed the street in front of the bar. Amy moved the slider on the screen to the point out where she entered the bar.

"This is where I arrived to take over Jennifer's shift." Amy pointed to the screen where it showed her entering the bar. "I think Jenny left five or ten minutes after I arrived."

Amy entered in the time and the screen jumped. She scrolled the time bar and the officers saw Jennifer leave the bar. Amy allowed the video to play showing Jennifer walking down the sidewalk and rounding the corner to where she had parked. After a moment, the video showed her walking back into the bar.

"That's right, I remember. She came back in because she forgot her cell phone," Amy interjected.

On the screen just off the street and out of the light of the camera, a shadow moved quickly along the road. One officer addressed the other, "Do you think that was him?"

"I think it was," Conners said.

Amy asked, "Who are you looking for?"

Jennifer exited the bar and rounded the corner. A minute later the headlights of her car pulled up to the street and turned right disappearing out of the camera's vision.

"Can you go back and play that again?" Conners asked. Amy scrolled back the video to when the shadow walked across the street. Conners looked at the other officer, "What are the heights on the two guys?"

The officer looked down into his notebook, "The Portland guy is almost 6'4" and Steven is about 5'10"."

Conners peered at the screen, "Well, that doesn't look like a guy who's almost six and a half feet tall."

Amy looked at the screen, unsure what they were looking for, "Who do you think it is?"

"Would you mind giving us a shot of the bar before you arrived?"

Amy keyed in the changes and the screen updated. The monitor now showed the bar counter where Jennifer was working. Ahead were a number of people enjoying their drinks. A man got up from the back end of the bar and walked down the line towards the camera. He turned and disappeared under the camera's view.

Conners pointed out the screen, "Can you pause it here?"

Amy stopped the recording and looked up at the monitor. "Who is that?"

Conners turned to the officer, "Do you have a photo?"

"Yeah, it's here in my notebook," the officer fanned the pages, pulled the image, and handed it to Conners.

Conners raised the image to the monitor so that the faces could be compared, "I think that's Steven."

"I agree," said the other officer.

They let the video play through and they saw that Steven left shortly before Jennifer got off her shift. They flipped back to the camera outside and they saw that Steven exited the bar and went off camera. The footage looped back to show Jennifer returning to the bar and the shadow figure crossing the street to where her car was parked.

Conners broke the silence, "Do you think we would be able to get a copy of this video?"

"I would have to ask the owner, but I don't see a reason why not," answered Amy. "I will let him know and we can send it over to you in a day or so. He knows how to save the video, otherwise, it overwrites the old video."

Officer Conners reached into his back pocket and pulled out his business card and handed it to Amy, "Just contact the department and let them know it's for me and they'll run the video into evidence."

Amy quietly held the business card in her hand, "Do you think she's ok?"

Officer Conners looked down, "I don't know, but we're looking, and that is best we can do right now. If you hear anything or if you remember anything else please let us know. You have my card."

The three officers thanked Amy and walked out of the room down the bar and out into the night.

Amy slowly sat down in the chair and put her arms on the desk. She stared across the room at the empty wall. She pulled out her cell phone and opened up a text message. She typed in Jennifer and composed a new message to her. After hitting send, she turned the screen off, put her head into her hands, and began to cry. Somewhere along a dark country road, a phone sitting in tall grass buzzed to life. After a moment, the screen went dark and the message was lost to the night.

CHAPTER SIXTEEN

"I'll be there within the hour." Vadym ended the call. He stood quietly in the small kitchen. The house was dark as his wife and son slept down the hall. His finger stroked the wipe cloth on the sink edge as he waited for the address to be sent. His breathing was steady and deep. The phone buzzed to life and he read the message. He swiped and sent a response. He placed the phone down on the counter and rubbed his forehead with the palm of his hand, as he arched his back opening his chest to the ceiling. His lungs exhaled in a deep sigh as he walked across the room and down the hall.

He entered a small room and flipped the light switch. A ceiling light turned on and the fan blades began to spin slowly. The walls were lined with dark wood bookcases stacked with old novels and magazines. Across the room was a desk that contained stacks of old notebooks and papers. He crossed the room and reached behind the open closet door. His arm lifted out a dull green military duffle bag. He placed the bag across the desk pulling the chair to the side.

Vadym returned to the closet and pulled down two storage boxes. He opened the lids and pulled out a roll of clear plastic and a bundle of tools. Both items were placed in the bag. He then placed a container full of surgical gloves and gowns as well as a rain set. He reached down and pulled open the main drawer of the desk and rummaged through. His arm moved through the material and pulled up a small collapsible saw.

From behind Vadym, a small hand rested on the doorknob. The weight of the child's body pushed against the door causing it to release a soft creak. Vadym spun around still holding onto the saw. The boy's voice was soft as he rubbed the sleep from his eyes, "Daddy, why are you up?"

"Pash, go back to bed."

"The light was on."

"Go back with your mom."

"She sleeps too loud."

Vadym's patience was waning as he walked over to his son, kneeling before him, "Go back to sleep. Lay with your mamma."

"What is that?" The boy motioned to the saw in his hand.

"Daddy is just cleaning up his office." He stood and walked across the room placing the saw into the bag. He turned back to his son. He reached down and the boy was in his arms. He rested his head against his shoulder as he entered the master bedroom. A woman was sleeping in the bed covered by a light sheet and wearing a cream slip.

The father leaned close to his son's ear, "Go with mom."

He lowered the boy into the bed. He carefully lifted the sheet and pushed the boy close to his mother. Instinctively she slid over and placed her arm around the boy. The two were fast asleep before Vadym made it back to the office.

He continued to load up the bag and carried it out the back entrance of the house. He reset the alarm and walked out of the house along the driveway to the garage at the back of the property. He passed two parked cars and entered through the side. He pulled the key out from the cabinet shelf and tossed the bag into the trunk of the car. He reached up on the wire shelf and pulled down a stack of storage bins and a large bottle of bleach. From under the back cabinet, he pulled a new set of boots fresh out of the package and placed them in the car. He fell into the driver seat and turned the ignition. The car was only used on special occasions and struggled on its first two attempts. The car woke to life and Vadym turned on the head lights and pulled out of the driveway speeding off down the street. The garage door slowly lowered behind him finishing its ghostly action alone.

CHAPTER SEVENTEEN

Jennifer sat silently against the wall of the room. Her back leaned against the open drywall and she rested her head against a cold stud. Her head hung down providing relief to her hands bound behind her. She squeezed her fingers together and pulled, but there was still no give. She felt a numbness as she rhythmically clicked her fingernails. Above Jennifer's head, light showed through the dirty window. Dust danced, floated, and swirled on the light beams. She had been lost in the hypnotic movement. Feeling her own mind drifting through the air. Across the room laid the motionless body of the man with his feet buried in stacks of papers and trash. Her eyes purposefully avoided the scene.

Jennifer took in a large breath and began to slowly slide her way towards the door. She balanced using her arms pulling herself backward through the room. She reached the wall along the door and peered out into the hall. The light from outside moved through the front door windows, illuminating the grain of the wood molding. She saw the marks made on the floor from the man. Channels were carved in the dust through old footsteps and handprints.

Along the base of the wall were crumpled baggies and syringes. The accumulation of lint and dust revealed their age. Further down the hall, she could see the house open up to a living room. Along the side of the hallway, a half wall formed a darkened cave. Jennifer peered into the darkness as two eyes slowly opened and stared down the hall towards her. A woman was huddled in the corner covered with a rotting blanket. Jennifer could see her eyes moving in rhythm as her head bobbed and shook gently. Her face was cuddled in the blanket obscuring her nose and mouth as her long greasy hair flowed down her side.

Jennifer stared at the woman and whispered through the cut in the tape, "Help." There was no answer. She repeated again and lightly rapped her head against the door with a hollow thud. The woman clenched her body as a shiver took over. She looked up slowly to the entryway. Jennifer repeated her call and knocked the door again. The woman continued to pan across and meet Jennifer's eyes. They were heavy and sunken and she made no movement. Jennifer continued to speak out to her but there was no reaction. The woman was distant and empty. Jennifer stopped her efforts. She knew there was no hope with this vacant creature. What was this place, Jennifer thought, and why had they dumped her into this home with these people?

She rested her head on the door jamb still staring across at the woman. Her eyes quickly shifted to the main room. They widened and Jennifer could see the bloodshot whites of her eyes. Her head sank further into the blanket and she pulled back into the corner. Jennifer felt a slight tremor beneath the wooden floor and a stomping sound from the hallway. With her knee, she closed the door to just a crack. Her single eye peered through the opening as a tall lanky figure stumbled into view. He swayed unnaturally in the hall, his thin legs protruding from torn shorts. He stumbled and continued on to an adjacent room. Panicked breathing took over again in anticipation of confronting another person. She had dealt with the man on the floor but he didn't move with the same force. The man walking down the hall could have his way with her. She closed the door to the room and slid over to the trash. She kicked an empty box against the door and moved back to the corner. At a minimum, she wanted to know if someone were to walk into the room. Not that it would make a difference, but she didn't want to wake up to a fresh face staring at her.

For a while, Jennifer stared at the doorknob expecting it to turn and reveal the man from the hall. The minutes rolled by and the house remained silent as Jennifer's mind began to relax. She thought her of her grandmother sitting on the couch watching television and laughing about the day. In that moment, she regretted being so aloof in her phone conversation in the car. She would give anything to see her again and talk about stupid shows, to see her friends at the coffee stand, and serve drinks at the bar. She wished for the mundane tasks of washing glasses and swiping credit cards, hearing the harmless flirting and obnoxious drunks.

Her mind drifted to the cruise boat. It would be the first vacation since driving with her family to Disney. She had seen the cruise brochure at a diner about a week after arriving at her grandmother's. Her bruised eye was still hiding behind her sunglasses as she waited to be seated. The images of the rooms, piles of food, and the happy people dancing on the deck. She wanted to be there. She knew it would be a struggle, she had always fought money. They were on and off friends. Living down in Portland with RT meant she didn't need to think or worry about money or responsibilities. Her grandmother had set rules for moving back in and Jennifer had no choice but to adhere. It was hard going in the first few weeks. She struggled to find jobs and accept the monotony of her new daily routine. It had been months and she was, only now, finding her path. Her grandmother even noticed and told her to do something for herself. Jennifer had saved the brochure and brought it up one night after dinner. Her grandmother agreed that it would be good for her to go and encouraged her to start saving.

Sitting in that room bound by twine and tape she could still dream of the trip. She could see herself standing on the balcony wrapped in a blanket, sipping a drink and watching the misty blue morning rise in the Alaskan fjords. She could taste the coffee as she licked her lips through the tape on her mouth as her hair blew in the breeze. Her bound hands rested on the railing. She smiled as she heard seagulls flying overhead and the boat moved through the black water. The light in the dream began to fade and the sound of distant popping gravel and headlights pulled Jennifer into reality.

Above Jennifer's head, a beam of light shone through the window and cast shadows on the wall. Light shadows moved from left to right as the car turned up the drive into the front of the main house. Jennifer lifted herself up against the wall and craned her neck. Her head met the windowsill and her right eye could see high enough to view the car shifting into park. The headlights turned off and the door opened. A thin young man stood up, shut the door, and quickly trotted up to the front of the house and walked in.

Jennifer slumped down to the floor and stared out across the room. With the arrival of a new person, she renewed her attempts to break the bindings. She quickly scanned the room and saw the power cord stretching out from the trash pile. She slid over to the pile and began to kick. What emerged was a shadeless lamp. She saw the light bulb at the end of the lamp. She shifted her body and lifted her legs. Her feet came down smashing the bulb. She paused, her ears searching for any hint of discovery. It was silent. Her body shot around and she began to saw at her bindings with the protruding glass piece. As she rocked her hands back and forth, she could feel the glass on the ground grinding along her fingernails and wrists. Sharp stabs of pain went through her fingers as she moved too quick catching some glass across the skin.

Jennifer was cutting when she heard the pop of the screen door on the neighboring house. A male voice was talking and it was growing louder by the moment. She paused and turned her head to the window. The voice was moving in her direction. A man was on his way to the house. She doubled her efforts and moved with a passion. Her hand nicked the glass pieces causing her to wince as small trickles of blood ran down her fingers and onto the floor. She could feel the bindings starting to fray and break.

CHAPTER EIGHTEEN

Nick pulled up to the house. He reached into the back of his car and pulled a small duffle bag into his lap. The bag contained two handguns wrapped in a shirt along with a magnetic metal box. Nick's paranoia had increased over the last few weeks when delivering finished units for distribution. His job was delivery to and from the house. As it was explained to him, "You're a jackass. Understand? A car mule. Drive slow, drive responsible, and always deliver. You're an in-and-out man. Raw product in, finished product out." He took the liability and risk in transportation. His deliveries had been increasing in size and value along with his paranoia. For Nick, a hundred grand of drugs in the car increased the risk of bodily harm, and the guns were his way of cooling that fear. The box was a tax on transportation. A skimmer by nature, he felt he deserved more than his normal wage.

He sat for a brief moment staring forward at the collection of cars and the flickering porch light. He pulled his hand to his face and took the last drag of his cigarette. He flicked the butt out of the window, the orange end glowing and spinning in the night. He was late to work and he knew he would get an earful from Tyler. His teeth pulled back on his lower lip and he closed his eyes. His finger pulled back on the lever and the window began to roll up closing him in. He opened the door and quickly walked up the porch with his small bag in tow.

"Sorry I'm late," he said clearing a small path between bags and boxes. He lowered his head preparing for the onslaught that never came.

From the other side of the room, Tyler coiled his body to see Nick, "I need you and Steven on bud sorting and med setup." Nick's face softened to Tyler's tone. The verbal beating never came. He shifted between Steven and Kora who had not turned to greet him. Their heads were down and busy cutting material, processing, and bagging.

"Good evening to you all too. Lover's quarrel?" His arm arced the room. His sarcasm was ignored as he dropped his bag against the wall. There was a dull clattering of metal on metal as the bag settled. Everyone was too busy working to notice the odd sound.

"You're fucking late," Tyler said. Nick's mouth curled slightly. He knew Tyler would have something to say.

"I'm here now, amigo."

"Where have you been? You knew when we were starting tonight. I tell you that time and you need to be here at that time or you don't have a job."

"Hey man, I know I'm late. I fell asleep this afternoon and woke late. I got my shit together and hurried out, but I had to drop a friend off and it took longer than I anticipated. I was texting Kora to let you know. Hey, that's responsible right there. I didn't keep you in the dark."

Tyler was now fully turned and facing Nick, "You're a shit liar, Nick. There's a fucking child's art painting on your face."

"Hey, I'm telling you the truth, but I'm here. Just forget about it. Time to sort some bud, right? I am on it. Bud, bud, and more bud. I love sorting bud."

Tyler saw his arms and his palms lift to the ceiling. It was Nick's tell and Tyler's blood began to boil. He crossed the room and pressed Nick up against the wall. The kitchen fell silent as Tyler commanded full attention. "I can't deal with your childish shit tonight. I've got more to deal with than you can imagine and I'm not going to blow cycles listening to you. You will not be the next spur in my ass."

Nick's head turned, not making eye contact, "Alright man, I'm here. Let's just do some work."

Tyler backed off and navigated his way through the kitchen mess to the counter.

Nick looked at the back of the three heads in the kitchen. "What's going on tonight? Y'all look like you're pissed off or something. Are we getting shares cut or having to pull doubles again?"

Tyler's head didn't move as his hands continued to scoop fine powder form the mixing bag into small marked wax baggies. "This fuck," Tyler blindly pointed to Steven, "decided it was time to play bandito."

Nick's face showed a confused look, "I'm not following."

"The fuckhead here decided to take a lady and bring her to the office."

"What? There's a woman here?"

"Yes."

"Where is she?"

"We put her in with the heads and someone is coming to deal with her."

"What guy? She's with the heads? You put a stranger, a woman, in with the heads? Oh, that is low man. Those shits over there are insane." Nick's eyes opened wide as he scanned the room.

"A guy is coming to deal with the situation."

Nick's face started to open up and a deranged smile came across his mouth as his tongue played with his teeth, "Tyler, let me go see her."

"No, fucking sort bud."

"Tyler, one minute, man. I'll cash in on my first piss break, no biggie. I'll be right back." Before Tyler could respond, Nick was halfway out the screen door and onto the porch.

"A lady in our midst." He walked around the corner of the porch and onto the walking path. He mumbled in crazed excitement as he walked through the grass. His eyes lifted to the darkened house. He bounded up to the porch but caught his foot on the top step. His arms went forward and his other leg caught him on the wood. His hands scraped across the worn wood and he let out a gasp. His stumble released a loud thump as he tried to stand again. He walked up to the door. His hand pulled out the cell phone and he flipped on the flashlight.

The door creaked open and he shone the light down the hall. Slithering bodies moved in fear of the light. The tangled limbs pushed against empty walls and stripped flooring, stammering and clawing for relief in the darkness. Eyes hid behind dirty clothing and pulled blankets.

"Fucking animals." Nick scanned the hallway for any hidden bodies. He had always been nervous going into the head house. At any moment a body could stumble through a room or doorway grabbing onto a shoulder or leg. It was more terrifying than dangerous. The bodies were weak and easy to defeat, but the stress on the heart as it lifted to the throat was another thing altogether.

He looked left and right and saw the closed door. His hand reached the knob and he opened it. Behind the door boxes and paper pushed against his approach. He forced the door open as papers dragged beneath. The room had more light than the entryway. He could see a woman kneeling with her arms behind her back in the corner of the room. Her eyes were wide and she was breathing quickly.

"Hello there. How are you?" Nick smiled and entered the room. He closed the door behind him and in doing so, saw the body laid before the closet. "You have been busy tonight?"

Jennifer's eyes were terrified of this new figure. Her breathing was rapid and she released soft whimpers through the slit in the tape across her face. Nick crossed the room and stood before the man face down on the floor. His foot went out and lightly kicked the man. His skin jiggled but there was no response. He strained to view the man's face and noticed the dent in his forehead. Nick looked at Jennifer, "Feisty one."

Nick crossed the room slowly, shining his cell phone at Jennifer. She pushed her legs against the floor driving her back into the wall behind her. Her voice whimpered.

"What is your name, sweetie?" Nick began to lower himself in front of Jennifer. She kicked out with her bound legs but missed Nick. "It's alright, we'll keep our distance."

The light shone on her face and she recoiled turning to the open wall. Nick lowered the light down across her body. He stopped briefly on her pants and shirt.

"You're a pretty one," Nick smiled as he ran his tongue along the bottom of his lips. He reached down and grabbed the bindings around her feet and pulled her towards him. Jennifer's body sprawled out on the floor as Nick quickly straddled her, sitting on her thighs. His weight pressed down on her body compressing her arms behind her back as she let out a scream. The house awoke to the voice and returned the night's call.

Nick dropped the phone next to Jennifer, hiding the light. She looked up into the dark room to see the silhouetted man straddling above her. She tried to kick her legs but his weight held her down. She arched her shoulders and bucked her hips beneath him. He braced his arms to keep from rolling over.

"It's ok, it's ok. I'm not going to do anything to you. I just wanted to say hi." Nick now lowered himself down onto Jennifer's chest. The weight pressed the air out of her lungs. Nick's face moved inches from Jennifer's. She strained her neck to gather distance as Nick lowered his nose to her and took a long drag, "You smell nice."

His left arm braced himself over her shoulder as his right began to move gently down over her chest. He traced the bra line under the shirt as a single finger ran the profile gently flicking her nipple and moving onto her stomach. Jennifer's eyes were tearing up as her head pulled away. His hand ran down her stomach to the waistline of her pants. Her shirt had lifted and Nick's hand opened to touch. He began to run his hand under her shirt feeling the soft hairs along her stomach. He could feel a tremble ripple through her body.

From behind Jennifer, her unbound hands bled on the ground but were free to move. She had noticed the Leatherman on his left hip when he entered. Nick's hand was busy tracking up her shirt as she pulled out her right arm and gently put her fingers on the tip of the Leatherman. She waited for a pause as his hand reached the lace. She kicked her legs up distracting him for a moment. She lifted the Leatherman and returned her arm to her back. Nick reached for the floor to steady himself after the surprise move. Her fist closed tightly on the Leatherman.

He lowered himself again, "You've got some kick, girl."

She waited a moment for him to close the distance before bringing the crown of her head to his face. She pulled in her legs and rolled again. He fell back to the floor holding his head.

He yelled out, "Bitch! You stupid bitch!"

Jennifer pushed herself back up against the wall, still holding the Leatherman in her grasp behind her back.

Nick pulled his hand back in rapid succession looking for blood. He saw none and grabbed his phone. "Stupid shit, you'll get yours tonight. A treat is coming for you."

The anger welled up in him as he gazed into Jennifer's eyes. She was bound and crumpled unnaturally on the floor slowly inching her way into the corner. The flaring of Nick's nostrils signaled that the attack was not over. Nick pulled back his lips, his teeth shone brightly in the evening light. His fists curled and the veins in his arm pulsed with anger. He came at Jennifer with his legs, keeping his distance from her. He connected with the point of his shoe on the small of her back grazing her arm and the hand that secretly clutched the Leatherman. She released a terrified cry as the pain rolled over her back and across her chest. She felt a numbness down her legs that raged into a warm fire and then open pain. She felt for the first time tonight she may not survive. Nick's eyes raged as he growled. His foot reached up and he stomped down on Jennifer's knee. As if by reflex, she pulled in the throbbing knee and kicked out at Nick. She caught his left leg and he stumbled onto the pile of garbage. His hands reached out to brace himself against the fall. Jennifer defiantly screamed through the tape and reared back striking Nick in the thigh. He fell over into the garbage but quickly rose.

Before he was upon her, the door to the room burst open and Steven appeared in the entryway. Jennifer pulled back. Her face slowly gave way to horror. She was managing to keep one monster off her, but the sight of a second was insurmountable. She pressed herself against the wall and began to prepare to use the Leatherman in her hand. She opened the knife hoping this little weapon may afford her some chance at escape. Her eyes trained on the door as she waited for her moment to cut the bindings on her legs.

Steven looked at Nick who was lifting himself from the garbage still holding a hand to his head. He was screaming obscenities at Jennifer and preparing to launch another attack at her. Steven crossed the room and grabbed Nick by the shoulders and threw him to the opposite corner. "What are you doing? I could hear you from the house."

Nick curled up, defeated and licking his wounds, "I came in and she attacked me."

Steven glanced quickly at Jennifer and back at Nick, "She is bound and gagged. You're telling me that woman attacked you? You're really admitting that you got your ass handed to you by a helpless woman?"

Nick didn't make eye contact and Steven knew he was taking advantage of her. He looked back at Jennifer and took a deep breath. For the first time, Steven took a long look into her eyes. He could see the terror and abuse she had suffered. He knew this was all because of him and it made him sick. More so than the shootings earlier tonight. At least there he was trying to protect himself. He had convinced himself that the shootings were justified. Self-preservation and self-protection were the words that fluctuated through his mind. But Jennifer was a different story. He had done this and he regretted it. He jeopardized his job within the organization. How many crimes had he committed that night? He was sure someone must be looking for him. He didn't know which one was worse, Juan and his posse, or the cops. At least the cops would stop looking after a while, he knew Juan wouldn't.

He relaxed his body and for the first time that night, Jennifer calmed. She saw Steven's face full of remorse. It didn't change anything in her mind, but she was relieved her immediate nightmare was over. Steven looked back at Nick, "Get your shit and let's get out of here."

Nick got up, dusting his pants and straightening his shirt, "She was lucky and caught me in the leg."

"Why was she kicking at you? What were you doing?" Steven pushed Nick out of the room and closed the door behind him.

Jennifer stayed silent in the room listening to their words as they left the house. Nick and Steven left the porch, Nick still holding his head. They took the direct route through the grass. The late-night dew left water streaks across their pant legs. They both stumbled across the yard discovering uneven ground and made their way back up the porch and into the house and kitchen. From outside the kitchen, laughter could be heard as the group mocked the wounded dog returning from the woods.

CHAPTER NINETEEN

Conners' hand rested on the coffee machine as he stared across to the wall on the far side of the room. A large image of a shield sat like a sentry guarding the rows of cubicles that spanned the police office. His mind drifted to the video from the bar, the shadowed image replaying before him. He floated out of the camera's vision and down just over Jennifer's shoulder as she walked back into the bar. He could hear the noise of the bar rise and fall behind his ears, his eyes forward as he moved down the sidewalk. Ahead of him was the blackness of the road and to his left a shadow rapidly approached him, his feet shuffling across the asphalt. The shadow was faceless as it crossed in front of Conners. He turned his head and followed the shape around the corner of the bar. It walked up to the unlocked vehicle, opened the door, and climbed into the back seat. A short head poked up from the backseat, staring out with white eyes piercing through Conners. From behind, the bar door opened and Jennifer left the bar with the noises chasing her out. She rounded the corner and walked through Conners. He could see the head in the back of the vehicle dip down as Jennifer fumbled with her keys, her phone in her left hand. She opened the door and a moment later the car roared to life making a quick turn and left Conners standing on the corner. From behind he could hear a faint voice calling out.

"Conners...Conners," the voice called out.

A hand was placed on his shoulder and his head shook, "Yes?"

"Your coffee has been done for a few minutes." The hand lowered from his shoulder. He saw the face of the janitor. Behind the man was a pushcart containing supplies, brooms, and buckets.

Conners looked at the cup under the machine. The cup was still steaming. He reached out and pulled the coffee out of the housing and lifted it to his lips. He took a sip, "It's been a long day."

"Well, I figured you were either getting a good start to the morning or you've been here too long." The janitor began to walk away, his voice lifting over his shoulder, "Regardless, you look tired and you should probably go home."

"Thanks, duly noted." Conners spun around and walked back to his desk, sat down and stared at the blinking cursor on his report. He took a long breath and pulled up to the keyboard and continued writing. He detailed the current state of the investigation. Inside his mind he regretted stopping for the night. He knew there was a woman out there and she needed their help. The statistics are always right. As time goes by their chances of finding her alive drop. They had pressed this evening trying to find her. Conners knew that officers were still out looking for Jennifer, but the police had failed to find any new leads.

He finished the report by dropping it into the network drive. He slowly lifted himself out of the chair and arched his back. Soft cracks could be heard emanating from his lower back and knees. He locked his computer and pressed the power button on his monitor.

The evening was cool and cloudy as he exited out into the gated parking lot. He pulled out his phone from his jacket pocket and saw the stream of missed messages from his wife. He couldn't remember the last time he ate anything that wasn't a cup of coffee, and from the context of the messages, there wouldn't be anything at home either.

The car pulled into the lit parking lot of the all-night burger restaurant. The building included wrap-around glass and Conners could see that he would be sharing his evening meal with a pack of strung out individuals. Their wide eyes followed him as he approached the building. A string connected to a bell signaled his entry. He walked up to the counter and a young man asked him what he would like. Conners ordered the same thing he always ordered, a double cheeseburger with light ketchup. The young man rang up the bill and let Conners know that it would be two minutes.

He nodded and walked back to an empty table. He fell into the seat and tried to avoid the sets of eyes staring. Conners pulled out his small pocketbook in an effort to seem uninterested in the situation. He pulled out a pen and began to annotate his notes from earlier in the day. He ran through the entire evening, looking for anything he missed that could help locate Steven. Officers had already been to his house and found two less than sober individuals drooling on themselves. His brother was missing and Steven's car was impounded. He felt there was still a chance to find Jennifer since Steven hadn't yet surfaced. He circled Jennifer's name multiple times.

From over the notebook, Conners saw a figure move and walk towards him. He continued focusing down as the man walked by and entered the bathroom. He was wearing a long trench coat and a small backpack across his shoulder. The man's step was irregular either from a limp or glazed coordination. He could still feel the eyes on him from the opposite table.

His burger was delivered to his table and he thanked the young man and took the opportunity to shoot a glance at the table. The group was talking softly amongst themselves as they gathered their rolling luggage and began to stand up and quickly exit out the side door. The bathroom door opened and the coated man exited still carrying the backpack. Conners glanced at the bag and saw it struggling under a new-found weight. He pulled on the strap with both hands as it hung low across his back. Conners' eyes followed the man as he left out the door in the opposite direction to the group. He looked down at his burger. He could see the cheese falling gently down the side, grease was forming a small pool beneath the bun. He took a deep breath and pulled out his phone. He quickly dialed the number for dispatch.

"Yes, this is Officer Conners. I believe there is a male suspect walking down 23rd Street North carrying a backpack that may contain drugs."

"Can you describe the man?"

"He is about six foot tall, wearing a trench coat, and carrying a dark green bag that is straining under some weight."

"Thank you, sir. I've alerted the local unit in the area and they will check it out. Late night for you?"

"I'm almost done, just getting some food and heading home. You have a good night."

"Same to you." The phone clicked and Conners put it away. The restaurant was quiet. From behind the counter, the two employees talked softly and above Conners' head, indistinguishable rock music was playing. He reached down and pulled off the top of his hamburger bun and carefully placed fries horizontally. He replaced the top and began to quickly eat his meal.

CHAPTER TWENTY

Nick's hands were covered with black latex gloves as he sat at the kitchen table staring down into the large garbage bag. To the right and left of the bag were clear sorting bins and piles of green bud. A lamp light sat over the garbage bag as he quickly lifted and sorted the bud from the bag. His fingers rolled as he observed the color, looking for any brown dusty mold. He sorted left and right working both hands in rapid succession.

After a few minutes, the garbage bag was empty and he dumped the trace dust and leaf material into the plastic container to his left. He took the bud from the other bin and placed it back into the garbage bag. He tore off a piece of duct tape, sealed the bag, and using a sharpie he marked the bag *Sorted*. He then placed the bag in the finished materials area just outside the kitchen.

"The sorted bud is here at the entry," Nick said.

"Did you mark the bag?" Tyler asked.

"Yeah, bag's marked. Is that going to the shop tomorrow?"

"I think it's going to the med store. Are you moving on to hash?"

"Yeah, I'm getting prepped now."

"Watch that color when you process. It was too green last time. Be careful to watch for that leaf material dropping out."

He returned to the kitchen table and pulled the empty plastic garbage bin up to the chair. From a black duffel bag, Nick pulled out a white mesh bag and placed it into the garbage bin rolling the top over the edges. Nick took the plastic bin that contained the sorted bud and dumped the contents into the mesh bag. Using a small brush he dusted the bin ensuring that all of the contents were emptied into the container.

Nick walked over to the fridge and opened the freezer door. He pulled out a white block of dry ice and turned back to the garbage bin. Using a small hammer, he broke the dry ice into small pieces. Nick turned on the fan in the open window as the steam began to roll out of the bin.

From behind the kitchen table Nick pulled up the black container and placed it on top the surface. He reached down and pulled up the mesh bag from the garbage can and laid the bag into the black container.

With both hands on either side of the bag he slowly began to rock the contents back and forth. A steady stream of steam poured out from the bottom of the bag into the plastic container. Hidden within the steam was a light, brown-green dust.

Nick lifted the bag to the side and fanned the steam out of the container. He reached over and flipped on the lamp and lowered his head to see the fine powder accumulating along the sides. He returned the mesh bag and continued to rock. He repeated the process three more times; each time, the fine dust accumulated.

The spent bud was emptied back into the bin to be sold as bulk waste. Nick flipped on the overhead light and pulled out a surgical mask lowering it over his head. He gently lowered a large painter's brush onto the sides of the container to clear the fine dust. He meticulously continued around the edges of the plastic container and gathered the dust into a pile at the bottom.

He removed the lids of the empty mason jars and placed them on the kitchen table. Taking up one of the jars, he pulled out an old library card and began to scoop the fine powder into it. He continued this process until all of the jars were filled. He then used a fine cosmetic brush to gather up all of the trace powder into a final pile. From his back pocket he pulled out a small plastic bag and dumped the remaining powder.

He placed the bag onto the kitchen island, "Tailings for the cooks."

"A treat for the next break," Tyler smiled. Steven and Kora turned looking at the bag on the counter.

"It's pretty green," Steven said.

"It wasn't the best bud and it seemed a little over dry. There's a lot of green material in there, but I think it will finish well."

Nick returned to the kitchen table and pulled out the heavy steel press. He removed the wingnuts and pulled off the top plate. At the bottom of the press he placed a piece of wax paper. He took one of the mason jars and using a chopstick, gently dumped the green powder into the mold. He placed another piece of waxed paper over the powder and lowered the top plate into place. He screwed the plate down and began to crank on the press handle. The press squeaked under the strain as Nick lifted the jack. Nick felt the resistance and pressed the lever two more times ensuring a tight fit.

Nick unscrewed the wingnuts and lifted the top plate. He remove the wax paper and pressed on the jack. On the top of the jack plate was a dark green brick of hash. Nick gently lifted the soft brick from the mold and lowered it onto a new piece of waxed paper. He folded the paper over the brick and moved the brick to the cardboard storage box.

He looked down at the press and saw some material caught in the corner. Nick reached down to his hip to pull his Leatherman out of the holster. His hand touched the holster to find it empty. His eyes shot to his waist and verified what his hand had already told him.

Nick began to look around the table and next to the chairs, "Has anyone seen my knife?"

"Did you check your bag?" Steven asked.

"I'll check," Nick said. He moved to the doorway where his bag was laid up against the wall. He lifted up the bag and began to run his hands through the contents. He couldn't find the knife in the bag and looked back to the kitchen slowly scanning the floor to see if it had dropped. He stood and lifted at the sorted bag, nothing.

"I'm going to head out and check my car. I'll be right back," Nick said to the room.

"Dude, finish up and we can find it later." Tyler's hand gestured to the small mountain of bud left to process.

"It's my dad's old knife. I need to find it."

Tyler's voice showed his irritation, "Fucking delays all day long. Just be quick and get your ass back in here. We," he motioned to the room, "need to finish soon. The first delivery is in a few hours."

"I got it, I got it. I'll be quick."

Nick put his jacket on and left the house through the foyer. Tyler's eyes followed him out. He walked slowly shuffling his feet along the gravel driveway. His back hunched and his knees bent as he scanned the area looking for a glint of metal. He reached his car and bent down to look under the wheels.

"Where are you?" he muttered to himself. He lifted himself up and opened the door, moving his hands along the inner seat and center console. He moved food wrappers and lifted spent Redbull cans from the cup holders. His eyes scanned the corners and cracks.

Nick stood again looking out over the lawn between the two houses. He walked to the grass and began to sweep his foot along the footpath. A light rain began to fall around him as the frogs sang in the distant creek. He closed in on the front porch of the head house when his phone rang. He pulled out the phone and turned back to the main house. Behind him, a shadow gently swayed in the window. The eyes stared into the back of his head and then disappeared in a flash.

"Hello?"

"Hey man, you done tonight?" said the voice on the phone.

"I should be off in a couple of hours."

"Are you scraping some product?"

"Yeah, I'll take some off the top when I'm making the drop."

"What we going to get?" The voice sounded excited.

"I think some soft hash and a few bags of dragon. Listen man, I've got to jet and finish up here." Nick continued to scan the yard in front of him looking for the silver handle.

"No issues, man. Should I get some people together?"

"That sounds good. I need 50 bucks a person to buy in. Maybe enough for four to six. I'll text you when I leave."

"I'll get some people together. See you then."

Nick turned to the dark entryway of the house. He walked up to the front door and paused for a moment. His eyes flowed down the porch to the dirty window.

His arm reached out and opened the door. His eyes were still adjusting to the darkness before him. He listened for movement in the hall, took a deep breath, and then entered the house.

He closed the door and for a moment closed his eyes to force his vision to correct. He opened them and quickly lowered to his knee as he heard a slight scraping sound. Ahead of him was a woman crawling slowly down the hall. Her hair swayed and dusted the floor as her arms pulled her forward. Her fingernails popped and scratched as she pulled herself along. Nick felt panicked. His eyes were wide and he scanned the hall for others. It was empty. The woman's figure was thin and her shoulder blades shifted and protruded through the light fabric on her back. The woman ignored Nick as she slowly passed him in the hall moving to the front door. She lifted her arm slowly reaching for the door as Nick kicked with his foot connecting with her body and slamming her against the wall. She fell in a clump as the air escaped her lungs in a moan. The woman's body tried to lift itself again but failed and curled up against the wall. A large smile came across Nick's face as he silently chuckled seeing the woman give up.

Nick slowly turned back to the door. He approached it slowly and gently turned the knob. The door opened and Nick entered the room. The trash was still piled up and the man's cold body lay motionless at the closet entry. He slowly lowered himself to the floor and scanned for the Leatherman. His eyes moved across the floor and to the corner where he left the girl. It was empty and he could see the bindings piled in the corner. Nick's eyes went wide, but he dared not move. He continued to scan the dark walls of the room looking for any shadow or shape that may be the girl.

From behind Nick, a slight creaking sound could be heard as the door slowly closed behind him. Behind the door, Jennifer stood holding a wooden rod from the closet. She gripped the rod-like a bat and held it over her shoulder. She took a step forward with the bat loaded behind her. Nick turned to the shifting sound and presented his head as the bat was lowered across his face. The rod depressed into Nick's skull as it broke in two. Nick fell to the ground and was silent. Jennifer lifted the broken rod above her and brought it down again onto Nick's side. A loud crunch could be heard as his ribs broke under the impact. The sharp end of the rod stuck into his side and blood began to empty out onto his shirt. Jennifer pulled again and lifted the rod but stopped at the top of the stroke. Nick was motionless in the center of the room as Jennifer lowered the rod, rapidly breathing in the dusty air.

The anger poured into Jennifer's face, her eyes narrowed and she lowered her face to Nick's body. The words strained out of her lips, "Fuck you, you shit." She spat on his face.

A moment passed and Jennifer began to calm her breathing. She held the sharp end of the rod out and lowered herself to Nick. The blood was beginning to pool around Nick's head and chest. Her hand extended out carefully and she felt down his pant pockets pulling out his wallet, phone, and keys. She checked the phone.It was a burner and the screen was locked. She tossed it back down on to the floor. She opened the inside of the wallet and placed the cash and driver's license into her pocket along with the keys.

She walked across the room to grab the bindings. She quickly tied dirty knots around his feet and hands. She whispered to him as she worked, "Maybe one of the people in this house might come in here and show you a good time."

Jennifer left the room, pulling the door closed with a click. She turned and her hand went to her mouth as she stifled a scream. The body against the wall was curled up but squirming in place. The feet and arms struggled against the ground as if trying to claw their way out of the house. Jennifer watched the sight, taking in the depravity. It was the woman from earlier. She was even thinner than Jennifer had suspected. Her hair draped along the ground and Jennifer could tell she used to be a beautiful woman. Jennifer quickly scanned the hall for any other bodies but found none. She turned out the front door and left the house.

She didn't know what time it was, but it was still dark and not yet morning. The night was quiet and she hid herself against the column on the porch. Her eyes moved over the long-grassed lawn and across to the cars parked in the driveway. The air was clean and smelled of wet pine needles and forest dirt. To the right of the porch were tall pine trees encased in blackberries and thorns. She looked to the left to see an open field stretching out. Shadowed apple trees stood ominously in the bare grass. The evening was wet and cold as bumps appeared on Jennifer's arms. She rubbed her hands along her arms and huddled her shoulders as a light breeze fell over her.

She knew she had to get out, but couldn't risk running into another person. Jennifer watched the main house as she crept around the porch and into the fields. Around the back of the house were piles of rusted metal and scrap. She reached her arms out to steady herself and moved to the back of the house. All light was now blocked as she stood looking out to the field. The moonlight above fought through the clouds giving a dull grey color to the sky. It was barely enough to navigate in front of her. She could see the dark silhouette of the hills around her. There were no lights anywhere and no houses that could offer help. She stood alone in the darkness.

To her right, back towards the house through the deep rows of naked alder trees, she saw a road off in the distance. A pair of car headlights could be seen twinkling through the branches. She could hear the very faint sounds of road noise. She reached into her pocket and fingered the car keys. She knew that the road was the way out. She turned back leaving the empty fields behind her and made her way back to the dark house stepping carefully through the soft ground and mud. Her eyes focused in front looking for holes or depressions in the ground. She could hear her feet squishing on the ground as water pooled around her shoes leaving footprints and marking her path through the grass. She reached the house again and looked up and was overcome with terror at the sight of a man standing in the window. She muffled a scream and quickly crouched, staring through the tall grass at the window. Her eyes adjusted to the distance and she could see it was the man from the hall. He was standing in the window swaying softly but lost in his mind. Jennifer couldn't believe that this place actually existed. She had heard stories about communal houses filled with people taken by addiction, but this house was filled with horrors - empty horrors - and ghosts. They were not human anymore. Her mind wandered trying to understand why this place was here, why these people chose to spill out in this manner. She shook her head and moved low to the ground avoiding his view, turning towards the porch.

She inched her way around the house and hid along the brambles. Above her, the trees swayed in the breeze and she felt pine needles falling from above. Her eyes fixed on the cars in the driveway. She didn't know which car was the man's. She looked at the keys and saw the Honda logo. The Honda was parked in the back and she assumed it had to be his since he was the last to arrive. She watched the main house for any movement in the windows or doors. She slowly followed the gravel along the driveway. Ahead she could see the opening in the trees where a small bridge crossed a creek. Off in the distance over the trees she could hear an early morning logging truck engine braking on the road.

From the trees, early morning music could be heard as birds called and frogs croaked. She took another look to the house to see if there was any motion. She lowered her head and took a deep breath. This was her moment to escape. She had this one chance to get away. She set off running through the open clearing alongside the driveway. The ground was uneven and she stumbled clipping a large tree root. She caught herself and grasped the keys tightly accidently pressing the unlock button. Ahead of her the car flashed in the driveway. She quickened her steps knowing she had revealed herself.

CHAPTER TWENTY-ONE

Vadym could feel the heat on his face as he stared through the warm glass at day-old chicken strips and barbecue sausage on skewers. Around the corner through the open window, the gas station attendant washed the day's dishes. He had white dusted through his dark hair, tattoos decorated his lower neck, and his ears hung with piercings.

His eyes looked up at the man and he called out, "Do you need me to get anything?"

Vadym looked at the man, "I'll take a sausage stick thing."

The attendant wiped his hands with a towel and tossed it over his shoulder. He came around the side of the counter and reached into the display. The heat lamp showed on his tattoos.

"Which one do you want?"

"It doesn't matter." The barbecue sauce dripped as the attendant placed the skewer into the paper bag.

"These things are good, but honestly, after 8 hours of them under the lights, the sauce starts to crisp up. I could eat them all and at the end of the night, I do." The man smiled at Vadym as he moved to the register.

Vadym nodded as he placed the contents in his arms onto the table. Duct tape, more gloves, and an IPA bomber.

"Looks like a party, man."

"A party for what?"

"Beer, duct tape, and some sausage. That sounds like a party." The man smiled, revealing his yellowed crusted teeth.

Vadym didn't understand the joke and didn't care either. His eyes and face showed nothing and the man's smile drifted. "I will also take 20 dollars on pump two and a pack of Camels."

"The white car?" Vadym stared into the man's eyes. There was a pause and silence, "Right, the only car out there."

The man paper bagged the bomber and the rest of the items into a plastic bag. Vadym picked up the items, opened the door with this back, and slid out into the night. The attendant continued to stare out as Vadym walked to the pump. He pulled the towel off his shoulder and pursed his lips before he walked away muttering to himself, "Fucking asshole."

Vadym tossed the items into the back of the car and began to pump the gas. He rested against the hood of the car and stared at the non-smoking sign as he pulled out the pack of Camels. The cloud billowed out of his nose as a lone car drove past on the valley road. He steadied his mind and focused on the task at hand. He saw the girl in front of him, her shape and her size. He could see the plastic on the ground, the red from the blood, and the touch of her hair in his fingertips as he packed her away. His boots were now muddy from walking the logging road and his hands sore from digging. The valley forest lands were quiet and empty. He enjoyed walking among the trees in the early mornings, listening to the wild sounds, and imagining being a bear wandering and rummaging. Finding that enjoyment from rubbing against tree bark, catching a salmon in a cold stream, and stumbling upon a shallow grave. The gas pump clicked and Vadym flicked the butt onto the ground.

He continued up the valley road east and through the mountains. The black hills rose up along each side of the road blanketing the valley and surrounding areas. Ahead of him along the horizon, he could see a crest of morning blue. The peaks of the mountains were covered in white smoky clouds. Tall pines poked through the edges of the cloud line creating a mesmerizing contrast. To his right, the river weaved and meandered. It teased the road moving in, out, and around empty fields.

Vadym's phone called out that the turn was just ahead. The green sign on the road reflected the headlights and the river rushed beneath, down along the embankment and over the gravel beach. He slowed the car and turned onto the gravel easement. The wheels popped and crushed under the shifting gravel floor. He could hear the creek rushing ahead bubbling over boulders and stones. The wheels of the car rumbled over the wooden bridge as he gazed up the creek line disappearing into the dark woods. Ahead he could see the driveway arch out from the lit house. He pulled the car alongside the parked cars. He turned off the car and headlights.

He opened the bag from the store and pulled out the bomber. Using the keychain, he popped the cap and took a long pull on the bottle. He placed it into the cup holder and pulled out the sausage skewer. Vadym took a sniff of the sausage and began to eat. He never enjoyed working on an empty stomach; it would make him too nauseous. He forced the last of the sausage down his throat and finished the beer.

He checked his phone and saw a new message, *thank you for your help tonight, you should see the payment.* He swiped and opened his phone. The bank app showed the money had been deposited into his account. He closed the phone and tossed it into the seat next to him. He rolled his head in a circle and arched his back in the seat. It was early in the morning and the physical work would be a chore. He rested in the seat and stared blankly at the front door preparing his mind for the coming task.

His hand went to the driver side door. As he pulled the lever, the door opened a crack and the car to his left flashed its lights. He paused holding the door and scanned the front porch. He couldn't see anyone. He continued to scan the property and through the window of the car, he saw a terrified woman sprinting across the yard.

Her feet kicked up dirt and gravel as she quickly closed the distance to the car. She was breathing heavily and her heart was pounding when she reached the car. Her hands fumbled with the keys as she struggled to open the door. She was panicking and her vision was focused only on the handle. She reached out to open the door when a hand closed around her hair and pulled her away from the vehicle.

She screamed out, "Let me go!" She kicked her legs into the air and reached back to fight the grip. It was no use as the man pulled, wrenching her neck back. She saw the backend of his feet as he dragged her along the driveway. She kicked up dust and dirt. Her fingers clawed at the ground for any hold she could find. She swung her elbows wildly connecting with the backs of his calves and heels. The impact caused the man to stop for a moment and regain his grip on her shirt. She was at his mercy as he dragged her to the house. The light was growing all around her as the cars shrank from view. She remembered the moment in the car, the rag to the face, being dragged away. She began to tear up as she fought. She had been so close to escaping and getting back to her life and her grandmother.

She hit the first step on the porch and was lifted like a rag doll into the air, landing on the porch floor. Her feet struck the wood and announced their arrival. The door opened and she was pulled into the front area. She leaned left to see the kitchen full of eyes staring at her and her companion. Their faces were stunned at the scene. She recognized all of them.

"Please let me go," she pleaded and sobbed. Spittle fell from her mouth and onto the ground where her face rested. She bawled and coughed out each word, "Please! Please! Why are you doing this to me?"

From behind her head, the voice called to the men, "Where's the key for the rooms upstairs?" Tyler stared blankly and frozen in place. The man in the entryway held his victim in his hand and yelled out again sending shivers down the three spines, "The key! Now!"

Tyler reached into his pocket and produced a small key ring and tossed it across the kitchen. The man caught the keys and reached down punching Jennifer in the head. She fell dark and laid on the floor in silence. He stood calmly and called out, "Which one of you is Steven?"

Steven stood in complete silence, terrified at hearing his name. He knew this man was bad. The last thing he wanted was to be singled out in the house. How did he know his name? He could see himself being thrown into a shallow grave to be found by a wandering pack of coyotes. This man was not only here for this woman but him too. He didn't want this to be his time, not now and not this way. He turned to Tyler and whispered, "What's going on? Please no."

Kora turned to Tyler who stood firm staring at Vadym. His answer was cold and firm, "Go help." His face turned to meet Steven's eyes, "This is your problem."

Vadym called out again, his impatience was increasing with each moment, "I will not ask again. Which one is Steven?"

Steven stepped forward. He knew this was his moment, it was punishment for his crime. "I'm Steven."

"Grab her legs. You will help." Vadym held her arms as Steven grabbed the legs. Her body was light as they lifted her and carried her through the living room and up the stairs. They reached the landing on the second floor and entered an open room. They laid Jennifer's body on the floor next to the bed.

Vadym stood, both men staring at the body. A light trickle of blood rolled down from Jennifer's forehead where Vadym had struck her. "We need to move all furniture to the walls and lift away the bed."

Steven looked up at Vadym's face while he coldly stared down at Jennifer. His eyes moving along her body as if a butcher assessing a side of beef.

From downstairs Tyler and Kora stared up at the ceiling hearing the commotion of the two men moving the furniture in the room.

Tyler broke the silence between them, "Kora, where's Nick?"

"I don't know. I think he went to his car to find his knife?"

Tyler looked at her and for the first time that night, he saw her as more than just a worker, "Sweetie, can you please go outside and see where he is?"

Kora was still transfixed on the ceiling, "Tyler, where did he get her? She was in the house."

"Hell if I know. Please go see about Nick. I don't want you in this house alone while that man is here." She looked into his eyes and caught a glimpse of his fear.

CHAPTER TWENTY-TWO

Vadym leaned over the banister as he heard the front door close. "Hey!" He called down as Tyler emerged, "Bring me a mop and bucket, and the bleach by the door."

Tyler looked down to the materials and saw the bleach, "Ok, I'll be right up."

The request unnerved Tyler as he gathered the supplies and climbed the stairs to the second floor. His feet creaked under the old wooden floorboards as he emerged onto the second-floor landing. He turned the corner and hooked the bucket on the banister. His leg leaned back as he caught himself from falling down the stairs. He gathered himself and took a deep breath before walking down the dark hallway to the open door and light.

He could see into the room as Vadym worked. They had lifted the bed and placed it against the wall. The cabinets and side tables were pushed into the corner and a tarp had been placed onto the floor. The man's silhouetted body formed a cross as he opened the sheet of clear plastic, and using a hand stapler, began to attach the plastic to the walls.

Tyler felt nausea come over him as his mind saw the woman's face. What had they condemned her to? What had Steven done to force this? He was sick but angry. Angry for being placed into this position, angry for having to be part of this world. He wanted to leave. He could just get into his car, take Kora and drive away. He stood in a daze not realizing that Vadym was now looking at him through the doorway. Tyler could not see his face, instead only the shape of the man and his arm perched against the door frame.

Vadym stared at Tyler. He had seen this face before. The shock and horror. He had long since gotten over his profession but he never missed an opportunity to extend the fear. He knew reputation was the best calling card. In these moments he always allowed his voice and accent to deepen. He got off on this. "What are you looking at?"

Tyler broke from the spell and dropped the bucket. The clanging of the plastic broke the silence of the hall. He quickly scurried to the ground to fetch it. He was on his knees when he looked up at Vadym. He knew he was not the only person to experience this point of view. He thrust up the items and Vadym took them out of his hands. He felt the rough skin against his hands, cracked and dry, from too much chlorine use.

Through Vadym's legs, Tyler saw two sets of feet. Steven was face down on the plastic, blood oozing out onto the protected floor.

"Is that Steven?"

"Of course."

"He was just supposed to help!" Tyler knew it was his responsibility. He had killed Steven. He had condemned him to this fate. He should have sent Steven away to deal with his own problems. But instead, he shared in this guilt as he incriminated everyone in this savagery. He fought back the tears, "Why did you kill him? You didn't have to do that."

Vadym looked back and realized that Tyler didn't know, "It was part of the arrangement. I've been paid and I need to do the job."

"I didn't ask for this. It was just the girl."

"Aw, he was your friend? Well I'm sorry, little ant. This is what the boss wanted."

"He didn't tell me this," Tyler's voice rose as he stood still, staring over Vadym's shoulder. "This is my crew. When I talked to him, he said Steven would only have to help."

"Well that wasn't the arrangement now. So, go along and do your job so I can finish mine."

Tyler backed away from Vadym. He wanted to escape this horror. Vadym walked back into the room slowly closing the door. His cheeks pressed up against his eyes with his teeth showing as he smiled. Tyler was left in the dark hallway staring at the door. He heard noises of objects being placed on the floor. He could only imagine what was happening and what would happen.

He struggled down the stairs held down by the burden and consequences of the evening. Like a ghost, he entered the kitchen and rummaged through a number of drawers before finding the bag of yellow ear plugs. He pocketed two bags for Kora.

He had tears running down his face. He wanted to embrace Kora. He wanted someone to hold. He wept in the corner of the kitchen still seeing those feet and Steven's dead face and the red blood. Tyler regained his composure as a loud noise came from the stairs. Vadym stormed through the house and out to his car. He watched this devil search for more supplies.

CHAPTER TWENTY-THREE

Kora pressed open the door and found two bodies sprawled out on the floor. One was bound and rocking gently on the ground while the other body was motionless face down near the closet. Kora dropped down next to Nick's body and placed a hand on him, "Nick are you ok?"

Her hand pulled back revealing a dark stain on the tips that smelled of blood. She scanned Nick's body and pulled the bindings off. Nick rolled onto his back and moaned.

Kora pulled Nick to a sitting position and pulled up on his belt leaning his tiny frame against her chest. Nick was small and Kora could drag him, bracing his arm over her shoulder. She carefully navigated the grass walkway between the houses while imagining how Nick could have gotten himself into his current position. Kora was never a fan of Nick so seeing someone get the best of him provided some enjoyment. After such a long evening, Kora welcomed any reason to smile.

She reached the porch stairs, opened the front door, and walked through the entryway as Tyler came rushing in from the kitchen. Tyler's face was lost in shock, "Jesus, what the hell happened?"

Kora laid Nick down on the living room couch and caught her breath, "I think the girl finally got the best of Nick. I would imagine we're very lucky she didn't get away. That is nasty right there." Kora pointed to the large welt on Nick's head and the dried blood trail down his face.

Tyler leaned in and examined the wound along his abdomen. "That looks like its still bleeding. Kora, can you check his bag to see if there's some clothes or something?"'

Kora whispered to Tyler, "We need to get him to the hospital. There is one in town."

Tyler shook his head, "I know, but we can't stop now. We've got a deadline to meet."

"Tyler, he's got an open wound on his side. We have to get him some help." Kora's voice cracked slightly as she stared at Tyler.

"I know, we need to stabilize him and finish up. Then we'll drop him off in an hour or so. If anyone drops him off there will be questions. You won't be able to just leave him at the front door of the emergency room."

Kora returned with Nick's bag and began pulling items out onto the table. Inside she felt cloth. She pulled and the two handguns fell out as the shirt unraveled. They struck the top of the coffee table. Both Kora and Tyler jumped as they clanked to the ground.

"Fuck." Tyler reached down and pulled up the gun. He checked the chamber, "They're loaded."

"What is he doing with those?" Kora asked.

"I have no idea." Tyler turned on the safety and gave one to Kora.

"I don't want it." Kora pushed back.

"Take it. I don't trust that guy upstairs and this is our best protection." She took the gun as Tyler pressed on the wound, blood pouring over his hands, "Tear that shirt up and press it on the belly wound."

Kora tended to Nick as Tyler rose and began to pace the room. His lips moved quietly and he shook his head.

Kora rose, "We need to get him to a doctor."

Tyler continued to pace, "We don't have time." Tyler's eyes shifted to the roof as he heard Vadym pacing in the upstairs bedrooms.

Kora's eyes narrowed, "What do you mean, we don't have time? Nick needs help."

Tyler slowed his pacing and turned to Kora. His eyes narrowed and his lips turned white as his anger boiled up, "I think it's clear we don't have time. In case you don't fucking realize," his voice dropped slightly, "we've got some guy upstairs setting up for God knows what because Steven decided it was time to play badass."

"It's not that way at all."

Tyler's anger raged as he pointed at Kora, "I don't give a fuck what you think right now. This shit is out of our control. We are only here right now because I need to finish this round and make this delivery. My ass is on the line and I'm here staring at one of my workers in dire need of medical attention and an absolute mess upstairs."

Kora put up her hands and pointed at the couch, "I know you're under pressure and things have gotten out of hand, but what we need to do right now is help Nick."

Tyler looked at the body, "How many more bodies are we going to produce tonight?"

Kora was quiet before she answered, "He wasn't the only body in that room. There was another. One of the heads."

Tyler's hands were shaking. Kora had never seen him this upset before. Tyler took a deep breath and calmed himself. "You're going to stay with Nick and I will finish the run."

Kora reached over and pressed down onto Nick's abdomen trying to slow the bleeding. The blood oozed through the shirt and smeared across Kora's hands. She looked down at Nick and gently spoke. "It's alright, Nick. We're going to get you to the hospital soon." She knew it was a lie.

CHAPTER TWENTY-FOUR

Dean's eyes opened and he stared up at the ceiling. He reached down and felt the pressure in his abdomen. The blood pressure medication was a diuretic and it would mean his third trip to the bathroom tonight. He carefully lifted the blanket and rose out of bed. He looked down to see his grandchildren sleeping soundly next to his wife. They had had a full evening of games, laughter, and food. He always enjoyed these weekends. He smiled as he turned to walk out of the dark doorway and down the hall to the bathroom. Halfway there, the pressure began to build and he quickened his pace. He burst through the door flipping the light and slamming up the seat. He was nearly late as he relieved himself into the toilet.

His eyes squinted at the pain and burning sensation. He finished and leaned his arm against the wall and rested his head. "Jesus," he said as his breath left his body.

The pain had increased from the day before and he knew a trip to the doctor was needed. He took a deep breath and flushed. He crossed the house and entered the kitchen opening the fridge. At the center was a half-eaten apple pie. He pulled down a plate and cut himself a piece. He grabbed the pack of cigarettes from the top of the fridge and walked out onto the back porch.

The air was cool and a gentle breeze flapped against his pajama pants. He placed the items down on the porch railing and went back into the house to fetch his jacket. He emerged onto the porch and zipped up the coat. He slowly ate the pie through his mustache as he stood in the dark staring out across the yard to the tall tree line. From behind Dean, a small scratch could be heard at the door. He turned and let out the old yellow lab. The dog stepped down the porch and began to sniff through the grass. Dean finished the pie and leaned against the porch column. He flicked open the zippo and released a cloud of smoke into the evening air.

Dean's eyes began to droop. He called out to the dog, "Come on, boy. Hurry up." The dog looked back and continued to sniff. The dog knew this was his five-minute warning.

Ahead of Dean, he could hear the gravel pop from an approaching car. The lab stopped and lifted its head at the passing car, its ears perked listening to the distant intruder. The orange light shown through the blackberry bushes at the edge of the property as the car continued off into the distance up the length of the tree line and parked at the neighboring house. Dean could not see the house that shared his easement but he could see the lights turn off as the car parked.

The dog slowly made its way to the porch as Dean collected the plate and lighter from the railing and waited for the lab to pass him into the house. He entered through the doorway as a faint voice rang out in the distance, "Let me go!"

He stopped and looked over his shoulder to the tree line. He narrowed his eyes and listened carefully. After a moment he heard the voice again, "Please let me go."

Dean stood quietly assessing the situation. He walked back into the house, closing and locking the door. He placed the dish in the sink, picked up the phone, and dialed 911.

CHAPTER TWENTY-FIVE

Jennifer's arms shifted on the floor as the plastic crinkled beneath her fingertips and stuck to her face. Her ears rang and head throbbed with pain as she raised her hand to her face to wipe away a thin line of blood. Her eyes opened and she struggled to scan the dark room. The light from the hall outlined the door and illuminated the smooth wood floorboards. Along the far wall was a boarded up window. She carefully stood up from the floor and tested the board strength. The boards creaked but would not give. Around the room, furniture had been stacked haphazardly. A nightstand stood precariously on a dresser and the bed was on end against the far wall smashed against the railings. Jennifer carefully opened the drawers. The old wood gnashed against the rusted railings as she reached her hand into the dark, her fingers feeling for anything but finding only dust.

Jennifer crossed the room. Her anxiety was taking over as her breathing rose and heart rate surged. The floorboards creaked under her toes as she carefully crossed the plastic floor. She could feel her heart in her throat beating as she reached out to the closed door. Her hand grabbed the knob and turned. She heard a click and she knew she was locked in. She lowered herself to the ground and peered out from the bottom of the door and into the hall. She could hear rustling and noises coming from the hallway. A small light illuminated the edge of the span and she could see a shadow moving quickly as if preparing for something. Her mind was still in the driveway, feeling the gravel drag beneath her hands. The pain as her hair was pulled out strand by strand and being thrown like a toy into the house. She remembered calling out for help but everything went black after that. She knew this shadow must be the man who caught her outside, that special surprise that was promised to her. She stared across the hall to see the staircase leading downstairs. Light lifted up from the first floor and lit the dark landing. She knew her only escape would be through the house.

Suddenly footsteps materialized and stormed down the hallway towards the room. Jennifer cupped her mouth to mask her breathing. Had he heard her? The whites of her eyes shone out the bottom of the door as the feet stopped. She could see the man's toes dancing in the boots. She could see the mud from the driveway, still fresh and wet. On the edge of the boot was blood smeared along the side; she could smell its metallic odor. Her face was at the door and would surely be hit if it opened, but she dared not risk moving for fear of drawing attention. She was supposed to be passed out on the floor not walking around. She could hear his labored breathing and the faint smell of cologne drifted down. The pause felt like an eternity before his boots turned and he walked down the stairs. The steps creaked and strained under the man's weight and she could see his pale cracked face as he disappeared beneath the railings. It was a blank face, muted and empty. Jennifer knew that she needed to assess her situation and prepare to leave. The face haunted Jennifer. It was a face of evil and she knew it would be back for her.

She stood and turned to the empty room, her shadow arced across the wall as her eyes scanned. She took a step and her foot bumped an object. It was a large black bag. She leaned in and slowly opened the top of the bag. The zipper popped against each latch. She could see a pair of dark pants had been placed across the top. Her hand touched the fabric and it was sticky wet. She pulled her fingers back and in the dark, she saw the wet stain dripping from her nails. She pulled the zipper again and in the faint light, she saw a clenched hand resting. She pulled further seeing Steven's face smashed against his arm. She fought the scream. She zipped up the bag and pushed back against the room shoving herself against the plastic lined wall. She frantically wiped her hand on her pant leg trying to clean herself of the horror she had touched. Tears streamed down her face as her mouth arched in agony. She got up and crossed the room slowly sliding down the wall, the plastic crinkled as she met the floor. She curled into a ball, holding her knees and silently poured out her pain alone in the dark room knowing these moments may be her last.

CHAPTER TWENTY-SIX

Conners drove down the valley heading home. He always enjoyed dropping the window and having the cold breeze blow through his hair. The rain had let up and he leaned back in his seat enjoying the open road. He pulled up his drink and took a sip. The day had been long and it would likely be an early start tomorrow. He was running excuses through his head to give to his wife when his shirt pocket began to vibrate against his chest. He pulled the phone out and answered the call, "Conners here."

"Good evening, sir. This is dispatch. We've had a call about a domestic disturbance in the valley east of Arlington. We don't have any units in the area and I was calling to see if you would check in on the call?"

Conners shook his head softly, "Is this urgent?"

"Sir, a man said he heard a woman cry for help."

"Any more information?"

"Just those details and an address. I've called in another unit but they are 10-15 minutes out."

"Send me the address and I'll check it out until the other unit gets there."

"Thank you, sir. I'll send it to your computer now."

The navigation system instructed Conners and he pulled onto the easement and into the driveway. Ahead was a man standing on the front porch. Conners exited the car and walked up to the entryway. "Good evening, or better yet, good morning."

"I think it is a good morning, officer. My name is Dean."

"Conners." They shook hands, "I got a call about a domestic disturbance that was reported?"

Dean nodded and went into his story, describing the car's arrival and the inevitable scream. On the porch next to him lay the old yellow lab panting in the cool morning air. Small traces of breath could be seen on each exhale.

Conners made notes in his book, "This is good information, thanks. There should be another unit coming soon to assist. Dean, what do you know about your neighbors?"

"The house was up for sale a while back and was purchased. There wasn't anyone using it until the last year or so. I don't know much except they tend to be quiet for the most part. I only see cars coming down the easement once in a while."

"Is it a couple? Or family?"

"To be honest, I'm not sure. I've seen some younger men driving up so they might be friends of one of the kids? I couldn't be sure."

Conners looked across the lawn and pointed to the tree line, "Just over the brambles there?"

"Yes sir."

"Alright." He put the book back into his pocket. "I'm going to drive by and take a quick look. I should be back when the next unit shows up."

Dean nodded and shook the officer's hand, "Thank you, sir."

CHAPTER TWENTY-SEVEN

Jennifer's mind was foggy and distant. She blinked quickly trying to clear the last of the tears from her eyes and focus on what was right in front of her. There was a dead body in the room. Steven's face was still seared in her mind. When she was bound and gagged in that house surrounded by those people, she had cursed him. She had wished the worst, but now she saw it. She had hated him, but seeing him reduced to a nylon bag was more than she could bare. The feelings of remorse caused Jennifer to tear up again. This experience was a nightmare. She wiped the drops from her cheeks with the back of her wrist.

Her head throbbed and she could feel the pulse in her throat. It was difficult to swallow and her mouth was dry. She ran her hand across her leg and she felt a lump in her pocket. She reached down and pulled out the Leatherman that she had stolen. She carefully opened the handles and lifted the blade. She closed the handles into her fist and she stared at the door's reflection in the blade. Along the handle was the inscription, *For My Son.* She sneered at the line. She gripped the knife, it was her only hope to survive. She did not fear using it.

She turned back to the door as she could hear footsteps coming up the stairs. She could see the boots at the foot of the door. She thought to herself that this may be her only moment to get out. Her hand squeezed the metal. She could feel sweat dripping down her palm. The plastic rustled as she stood bracing herself against the wall. From outside the door, she could hear the man taking deep breaths as if filling his lungs for a deep dive. The voice let out a guttural roar as the door was unlocked and flung open. Before she could see the man's face a light was turned on and she was blinded. Her eyes were still sensitive to the light and she lifted her arm shielding them from view. She could hear the steps crashing through the plastic floor. She peered through her arm to see the man charging at her, his body and face were covered by a surgical apron and mask and around his hand was a dripping rag. He was fast and came up on her reaching for her face. She instinctively put her hands out to block his advance and kicked with her strong leg meeting his midsection. She parried his attack. As the man fell to the ground clutching his waist he clipped her arm and the knife fell to the floor and slid against the wall.

The door to the room was open. She looked back for the knife but chose to bolt for the exit. Before she could gain any space a hand was on her waist pulling her back as she stumbled across the floor tripping on the plastic and collapsing into the open closet. She crashed against the wall impacting her head against the loose drywall. Dust coated her head and shoulders turning her a milky white. She quickly regained herself as the man jumped to his feet and reached for her. The man's veiled face haunted her and she released an ear-splitting scream. No one in the house could be ignorant of the actions on the second floor. He pulled her arms and threw her across the room. She sprawled across the plastic, her face grinding against the floor. Her body shook and cracked at the impact. The pain threatened to fold her up like a piece of paper leaving her exposed to her tormentor.

Before Jennifer could put her hands up the man was on her. She could feel his hot breath against her cheek as the wet rag was placed over her mouth. She fought and kicked taking in the fumes. Her arms flailed as he pressed down on her face. Jennifer arched her back and ran her arm along the wall. She reached and felt for the knife, straining as the man's face met hers. She felt her mind beginning to drift as the chemicals worked through her lungs and slowed her mind. She strained once more. As her consciousness slowly slipped from her body, her fingertips met the cool metal. She pulled out the Leatherman and drove the blade through the air.

Her eyes focused on the wrinkled outline along the side of Vadym's face. She snarled under the rag as time slowed. She saw his face slowly contort as her closed fist approached his face. Vadym braced himself against the coming blow, not seeing the point of the knife as it rammed into his face. The blade pierced his eye and continued through the soft flesh stopping as it reached his skull. She continued through the strike pushing Vadym's face back.

Jennifer's face was immediately covered with a clear liquid and thin drops of blood poured down onto her. Vadym fell back reaching for his face as the pain began to register in his mind. Jennifer quickly swiped the liquid from her face, smearing the blood like war paint. Her face was a soft red and the last of her breath roared out of her as she fell to the floor and heaved. The chemicals were too much and nausea rose in her throat as she released her empty stomach onto the floor. She stood, still heaving, and ran for the door. Jennifer dizzily planted her foot and twisted her ankle falling over the edge of the bed and onto the ground. She clutched her foot and crawled out of the room using the banister to lift herself up.

She looked back towards the room. The man screamed and writhed on the floor. The knife sat next to his face as blood ran between his fingers and down his crumpled mask. She wasted no time and began to limp down the stairs towards the light and into the living room.

She reached the base of the stairs and scanned the room. Tyler and Kora's horrified faces stared at her. They were witness to the soundtrack, the screams had shaken them, but what emerged was unexpected. Jennifer stood at the base of the stairs staring into the eyes of the man who sentenced her to a gruesome fate. Her eyes narrowed as the anger welled up. She gripped the banister tight and fought off the urge to lunge and continue her melee. She had suffered and now these people stood between her and her freedom.

Tyler guarded the entry as Kora stood alongside the couch where Nick's body lay limp across the pillows and blankets. She could not go through Tyler without a weapon. She looked to her right and saw the back door and realized it was her time to escape. From the very first moment when the gun was first placed to her head, she wanted an opportunity. She turned and rounded the corner. She pushed open the door and exited into the night. Behind her, she could hear Tyler's approaching footsteps and a muffled voice at the front door.

CHAPTER TWENTY-EIGHT

Conners emerged from the car slowly staring up at the house. It felt as if nearly every light in the house was on, illuminating the yard and the surrounding tree line. From over the house, the sky was beginning to show a light blue as the morning peaked over the valley edge. He closed his door and began to weave himself through the lines of parked cars. He looked across the overgrown lawn to the dark house tucked into the trees. He walked cautiously, carefully scanning the front seats of the vehicles. He didn't want any surprises and by the number of cars here he suspected that a party may be waiting for him.

He was halfway to the front steps when from the second floor through the walls, he heard screaming. He could tell it was a man's voice in pain. His hand instinctively moved to his side and he unbelted his gun and lifted it to his chest. As he climbed the stairs he could see through the glass window. A figure stood in the entryway staring into the house and across the living room. As Conners reached the door, the man sprinted across the room, pulling out a handgun from his pocket. Conners felt an immediate rush come over his body. His heart began to pound and his senses focused. *One man, maybe more.*

He quickly opened the door and yelled into the room, "Police. Freeze!" The man sprinting across the room stopped and spun meeting the officer. His face showed his shock as his arm lifted up and pointed. Conners wasted no time and fired at the man. The bullet ripped through his shooting arm and sprayed a mist of blood against the far wall. Tyler screamed out in pain and fell down behind a chair. Conners paused taking in the moment. There was an eerie silence in the room. From behind the chair, Tyler moaned out, blood beginning to pool around his shoulder.

"Drop your gun!" Conners cried out still seeing the handgun in Tyler's hand. He was breathing heavy and repeated, "Drop your fucking gun!"

Conners took a step towards the living room and emerged from the entryway. From his left, a shot rang out and he felt a tug on his leg. He fell into the kitchen and dove behind a counter. His empty hand went to his leg and pressed against the wound. His leg felt numb to the touch as the cabinet wood exploded about him. He closed into a fetal position and covered his head as pieces of cheap cabinetry and plumes of cocaine showered down over him. The shooting continued until the gun clicked empty.

Conners leaned out and saw the woman bent down behind the couch. He pointed and shot her in the stomach. She screamed out turning her face to the kitchen. Conners didn't recognize this woman. His finger pulled back again and Kora's body launched against the wall and slid down to the floor dead.

Conners cried out to the moaning man, "Where's the girl?"

He was answered only by moans as he heard the backdoor pop. Tyler's voice cried out, "No, don't!"

Conners cried out, "Where's the girl?" He peered around the corner fearing that Tyler had gotten away. Tyler's body was crawling across the floor and his arm was resting on the door trying to push it open. Blood had smeared a trail on the carpet.

Conners carefully stood feeling the pain shooting down his leg. He placed his weight down and walked carefully out into the living room. He scanned the walls and couch for any hidden people. He saw the man passed out on the couch, but all the shooting did not wake him. He swung around avoiding the staircase and walked up on Tyler.

"Where's the girl?"

Tyler's head turned and he began to roll. Conners

could see the black object as his hand emerged from under him, "Drop the gun!" Tyler didn't stop and Conners pulled the trigger again. The body fell limp on the floor. He kicked the gun away from the body and leveled his arms to the living room. The house was silent. Conners listened for any creaking or noises, but there were none.

He reached down and dialed his phone, "911, where is your emergency?"

"Office Conners, located east of Arlington at an earlier domestic call. There's been a shooting here. Three bodies."

"Is this at the location of the original call?"

"No, down the easement at the neighboring house. Lots of lights and cars."

"Yes sir, the ambulance has been alerted. Are you ok?"

"No. I've been shot in the leg but I'm stable."

"Yes sir."

From over Conners' shoulder and through the thin glass of the back door he heard a woman's scream. "I've heard a woman's voice. I have to leave to pursue." He never heard the dispatcher's request to stay as he dropped his phone, stepping over Tyler's body, and exiting the house.

CHAPTER TWENTY-NINE

Jennifer exited out the back door of the house, her feet leaving trails in the damp grass. She ran down the length of the house as her ears trained on the door behind her, anticipating the pursuit. Her ankle was still sore, but the rush of adrenaline carried her forward and her limp gave way to an open sprint. She reached the corner of the house and she heard a series of muffled voices and then gunfire. She fell to her knees covering her head and skidded through the grass. She looked back towards the door but it remained closed. Her mind raced trying to provide answers to what she heard. Where they shooting at her? She knew this was not the moment to wait and see. She lifted herself up and continued running towards the rows of parked cars. As she broke the edge of the driveway she again ducked as she heard a long barrage of shots coming from the house. There was a moment of silence and two more shots rang out. She captured her breath scanning the yard and hoping she was alone. She asked herself if they might be fighting inside the house. Could the man upstairs be shooting in the house?

Jennifer stared at the cars and scanned the windows for any faces. It was clear and she sprinted across the driveway to the open easement. As she passed the last car, she heard another shot from the house. She stood at the edge of the bowed gravel easement surrounded by brambles and willow trees. Above her, tall pines and cottonwood trees lifted into the sky and swayed gently in the early morning breeze. The branches made a clapping sound and for a moment it felt like the whole world was applauding.

Jennifer looked back at the house to see a stumbling shape moving through the grass. A hand was lifted to his face as he ran through the grass towards her. Jennifer processed the sight and her heart sank. A sickness swelled in her stomach as she realized it was the man from upstairs. He must have been shooting at the men in the house. He had removed the mask and gown and she could see the deep lines of blood running down his face and throat. His one good eye trained on her as he clumsily jogged across the driveway. Jennifer could not help but scream as she took flight down the easement.

Ahead of her was a winding gravel road that met up with the valley highway and bordered the main river. Her feet slid and stumbled over the large gravel rocks that formed the surface of the road. The road was not maintained and she weaved around the deep potholes that were filled with rainwater. Her eyes trained on the road ahead as she ignored the pain her body felt. She ran knowing just ahead of her was the main road, and all she had to do was flag down a passing vehicle. Vadym was close. She could feel his presence on her back, pursuing her down the road. She glanced back to see Vadym moving quickly. He had narrowed the distance and she could hear him panting.

"Come here," he cried out to her. The words hung in the air over Jennifer. Jennifer lowered her head and pressed on. Her feet plowed into the gravel as she willed her body to move.

The road lifted to a set of decaying rails marking the edge of a small wooden bridge. Below a deep swift creek poured over smooth river rock. The water boiled and undulated over the unseen terrain. The creek originated high up along the mountain ridge from the melting snowpack weaving through logging cuts and down through homesteads, ending into the main river bordering the valley road. Jennifer could hear Vadym's footsteps behind her. At that moment she realized that she would not make it to the main road ahead. She would fall victim to him on this easement and this time she would not be able to fight back.

Vadym growled behind her as he knew he was close. The only thought in his mind was retribution and punishment.

Her first step hit the bridge with a dull and hollow thud. The wooden boards gave and were weak from the weight of the cars driving over each day. She planted her strong leg into the groove of a wooden slat and she jumped over the old rotting railing. Her back foot clipped the edge and sent her tumbling into the creek. Wooden debris fell into the water as her body contorted entering head first.

The water engulfed Jennifer's body and for a moment, her mind reveled in the silence and peace of the stream. Her body turned in the water and her back gently bumped the muddy creek floor. Her eyes could feel the cold snowmelt as she opened them to the blackness. The early morning light could not penetrate the water and she saw nothing. She was wrapped in the darkness and for the first time that evening she felt safe and alone. Her body merged and rolled with the current as she was carried along.

Her arms reached out feeling the slick smoothness of the rocks running by her as bubbles flowed out of her nose to the surface. Her hands lost contact with the creek bed and she began to resurface. The peace of the water was broken when her head emerged. The air moved along her face as she was carried by the stream. The water bubbled and boiled all around her. She felt reborn. The water washed away the night and provided new guidance and purpose. She had a chance to survive.

She gasped for her first new breath, filling her lungs. Her chest lifted as she looked back to the bridge. Vadym stood, shocked at the turn of events. He was scanning the creek trying to locate Jennifer as she bobbed. The stress of running caused his eye socket to pulse fresh blood down his cheek.

A voice called out from the easement. He looked up the road to see a man carefully jogging down the easement from the house. He paused for a moment and his one good eye opened wide. He did not know this man. A voice called out to him to freeze. Vadym quickly scaled the railing and clumsily fell into the creek, releasing a terrible splash as a bullet struck the railing behind him.

Conners approached the railing staring off down the creek and saw two heads bobbing in rhythm. His leg screamed at him to stop but he pressed on continuing slowly down the easement towards the main road.

Jennifer heard the splash and the gunshot. She turned her body allowing her childhood swim classes to take over. Hanging willow branches slapped at her face as the creek flowed quicker around a turn. She reached out feeling the water for any unseen branches or logs that may slow her progress. Her belly lightly slid over the creek floor. Ahead Jennifer could see the rolling boil of a gravel bar. The stream was shallowing. She could not float through this section and she stood. Her knees pumped lifting her out of the water. The wet clothes hung on her body, dripping and adding the burden of extra weight. She could see the smooth deeper water ahead and began to sprint over the loose gravel. She reached the deeper section and dove into the creek. Behind her, Vadym ran through the gravel with his arms up balancing over the uneven ground. His head was turned revealing his good eye locked on Jennifer who was now in an open swim and gaining distance.

The cold of the water bit at Jennifer and she began to shiver as her body fought to keep her blood flowing. She couldn't stay in the stream any longer as she knew hypothermia would take its toll. She hurried swinging her arms, cupping her hands, and pulled herself through the creek. The raging water turned and opened to the main river. Above her head, she crossed under the valley road bridge. She could see the concrete footings on the river bank and the eroded walls lifted up to the road above. The rusted metal girders were bolted together and the green paint, long flaked off, was decorated with graffiti by bored valley teens. A large logging truck passed overhead loaded with fresh cedar from a cut deep in the mountains. It rounded the corner and the thunderous engine braking echoed along the dark walls of the valley. Jennifer could smell the cedar and she began to wince and cry. She knew that freedom was only a few feet away but the speed of the stream was too swift.

The momentum of the creek took Jennifer out into the middle of the river. She was a small dot barely distinguishable from a floating branch or clump of leaves. The immense river consumed her, hiding her location. The early morning light illuminated the banks of the river displaying the gravel islands with desperate willows clinging against the swift current. The river walls oscillated between sandy cliffs and gravel beds, meandering through the valley like a snake moving through the grass. It turned and swayed in a dance, giving land and taking shore. Homes were dotted along the edge enjoying its bounty and fearing its rage.

She looked back and could not see Vadym floating in the river. The river was raging and Jennifer could barely focus over the noise of the water. It was still dark and she could not make out any shapes in the water. The river was notorious for hidden trees and large boulders that would disappear her forever, or until the next flood loosened her body's hiding place. She told herself to remain quiet. Vadym could be anywhere.

She scanned back along the bank and saw a gravel shore jetting out and leading up through brambles to the valley road. In the distance, she heard the echoing sounds of emergency vehicles coming up the valley. Where they coming for her? Did they know she needed help? It would be a bad luck if they were to drive by, leaving her to die at Vadym's hands. She carefully coaxed her body across the current and towards the gravel beach looking out for Vadym who was hidden in the water somewhere in the dark boil. She fought the cold as her body tired against the strain. She swam through the water as her hands began to feel the riverbed. Her arms were numb from the cold and she struggled to lift herself out of the water. She emerged onto the shore walking stiffly through the gravel. Behind her, Vadym lurked in the shadows of the river.

She crossed the soft bed of gravel rock and hid in the tall reed grass line in the bank. Vadym could be anywhere. She hid with her eyes scanning the shore waiting for Vadym to surface. The sounds of the emergency vehicles grew louder as they approached. Jennifer knew if she could hold out that they would be able to protect her.

Her eyes and ears danced to every sound the river gave off. She was fooled by small waves and floating branches. To her right, she heard a crack among the rocks and her eyes darted like a frightened doe.

From the darkness, a voice broke through, "No one will find you."

Jennifer dared not respond for fear of giving away her position.

The voice continued, "You're close. I can hear you dripping."

The voice was so very close. Could Vadym see her? Was he just playing games? She continued to search with her eyes looking for any movement. The sounds of the emergency vehicles were nearly upon them. Jennifer could not see where Vadym was but she knew she had to get to the road and signal for help.

Jennifer broke her silence and between breaths and called out, "Help me! Please!"

Emergency vehicles were on the road. Jennifer could see the lights illuminating the trees and grass. The vehicles continued and turned down the easement.

Jennifer's feet touched dry rock and she pushed forward towards an open cut in the brambles. She continued to cry out as a rock connected with the side of her head. She fell to the ground into a clump of river grass, her body hidden from view.

She moaned as her arms reached up to the road. She screamed into the early morning light, "Help me…" her voice trailing off.

Vadym staggered above her, swaying, still dripping the river about him. His chest heaved with deep gasps of air. He pulled Jennifer's leg and she was dragged out of the grass with her hands tearing at clumps. She rolled to her back and through a dizzy fog she saw the shape of Vadym standing over her. He lowered himself and straddled her waist as Jennifer weakly pounded Vadym's chest. She called out, "Please no!"

Emergency vehicles had left down the easement to the house. The riverbank returned to sounds of bubbling water. Vadym laughed, "Help is on its way to you."

She sobbed and the tears began to fall from her eyes. Vadym reached to his right and pulled up a large rock and brought it above head. Jennifer's body and mind gave up, she had fought and lost. Her eyes closed and prepared for the swift end.

She never heard the shot but she felt the warmth across her face. Little drops of warm blood covered her as Vadym fell to her side. The rock dumped over his body and he lay still. She was in a purgatory, silent and alone. Was she dead, she wondered.

Her head was gently lifted and her cold body was pulled to the grass and cradled in Officer Conners' lap, "Jenny, we've been looking for you all night." She had no voice to share and cried in his arms. His voice leaned into her ear and softly soothed her, "You're going to be ok."

"Where did you come from?" was all that Jennifer could muster.

"From the house. I heard you." Jennifer believed him, feeling safety for the first time this night.

"Who are you?"

"Officer Conners."

Before her mind was lost to sleep, she glanced up at Conners and met his eyes lowering her head and whispering, "Thanks."

Conners smiled. He knew that the woman had been through hell, he could see it on her clothes. The dirt and blood mixed forming a timeline. He was relieved and spoke to her, "I'm happy to help."

Jennifer never heard this comment as she was already fast asleep. From the road above the bank, the red and blue lights came to a stop and men poured out stumbling down the river's edge to assist.

CHAPTER THIRTY

Everett Free Gazette
By: Mitchell Gretton
Title: *Miracle Woman Survives Drug Related Kidnapping*

Jennifer Lang's Friday evening ended like all the ones prior, she said goodnight at the bar and headed home at the end of her evening shift. That's when her night turned for the worst, as she was swept up in a drug related kidnapping that ended with four dead, two in critical condition, and over a dozen people arrested.

On Friday evening, Jennifer was kidnapped by Steven Pfeffer, a local drug dealer, and taken to a Lake Stevens bank where she was ordered to withdraw money to pay off a drug related debt.

"It is surprising, the callus behavior and lengths this man went to satisfying a debt," said a police investigator intimate with the case. "They nearly ended this young woman's life for about a thousand dollars."

The police said that they were already looking for Pfeffer who was being investigated in relation to a drug related shooting earlier in the evening when they believe he kidnapped Jennifer. Steven is accused of shooting two individuals that left a child parentless and in protective custody. According to the police, they tracked his car to a local Everett bar where they believe he kidnapped Jennifer. From there he held Jennifer at gunpoint, robbed her by driving to a local bank and withdrawing money from an ATM. He finally brought her to a house on Highway 530, east of Arlington, which was used primarily for drug production.

The police informed the Gazette that Jennifer was thrown into a neighboring house where she was bound, gagged, and tortured. The house contained almost a dozen people high on, what is believed to be, methamphetamines. The condition of the house was described as a "decrepit hazard", stating that there were bodies, drugs, and needles strewn everywhere. The Snohomish County Hazardous Waste Task Force is currently cleaning up the building.

The police have indicated that they believe the drug dealers were actively preparing to murder and dispose of Jennifer's body to hide the kidnapping. They found supplies in the house that they believe were going to be used to cover up the planned murder.

Jennifer was rescued when a neighbor called in a domestic dispute claiming to hear screams coming from the house. It was learned later that these screams were Jennifer's. The police responded to the domestic call and stumbled upon the house. Soon after arriving, the occupants began shooting. The police responded leaving two people dead. An additional individual was chased to the banks of the Stillaguamish River where shots were exchanged. Police confirmed he died near the river. All of the individuals were identified as members of a local drug ring. The body of Steven Pfeffer was also recovered. He appears to have been murdered and the police assume it was done by one of the individuals in the house.

Two other men were found in critical condition. The police are investigating if these men were victims or accomplices. The drug production house is believed to be part of a larger drug ring located in Snohomish County. A wide range of drugs were found including heroin, cocaine, and marijuana. The police estimate the recovered drugs have a street value of nearly $250,000.

Jennifer was treated for minor injuries to the head and arms, but has since been released to her family in Lake Stevens where she is recovering. Her family released a brief statement thanking the Everett and Arlington police for their help in this case and requesting the community pray for their family as Jennifer heals from her ordeal.

The police collected numerous vehicles, phones, and documents from the crime scene and are trying to piece together more information regarding the drug organization. Currently the police have stated that they are not making any additional arrests in this case, but have not ruled out a wider conspiracy.

The police do not believe that Jennifer was involved with the drug ring, but was merely in the wrong place at the wrong time.

The Everett and Lake Stevens Mayors have reached out thanking the local police force and expressing their support for Jennifer and her family. Everett Mayor, Tamara Nichols commented, "We battle every day to ensure our community is safe and secure. It breaks our hearts to hear of events like this, but we are blessed to have a police force willing to do what is needed to protect our communities."

THANK YOU

Thank you for taking the time to read my book. I hope you enjoyed the journey and are ready to continue on with more. It would be great if you could take a moment and head back to Amazon and give me a review. It really helps me to establish myself and for others to find the book. I wish you the best. Please head over to my website to sign up for my mailing list and check out what other books I have available.

www.matthewbuza.com
www.amazon.com

ABOUT THE AUTHOR

Matthew Buza is a part-time engineer, part-time farmer, and a full-time stay at home dad. He lives with his family on a small farm in Arlington, WA.

For more information on his writing and other projects, visit the website: www.matthewbuza.com

Yes, he enjoys Belgian Trappist beers.